PUFFIN BOOKS

A Dinosaur Called Minerva

Tessa Krailing was born in Kent and brought up in Sussex. She worked for the BBC as a TV drama production secretary, and later trained as a teacher. She taught mainly English and art before turning to full-time writing. She has written radio and TV plays and is a lecturer at Writers' Workshops. She now lives on the Isle of Wight.

A Dinosaur
Called Minerva

Tessa Krailing

Illustrated by
Mark Robertson

PUFFIN BOOKS

PUFFIN BOOKS

Published by the Penguin Group
Penguin Books Ltd, 27 Wrights Lane, London W8 5TZ, England
Penguin Books USA Inc., 375 Hudson Street, New York, New York 10014, USA
Penguin Books Australia Ltd, Ringwood, Victoria, Australia
Penguin Books Canada Ltd, 10 Alcorn Avenue, Toronto, Ontario, Canada M4V 3B2
Penguin Books (NZ) Ltd, 182–190 Wairau Road, Auckland 10, New Zealand

Penguin Books Ltd, Registered Offices: Harmondsworth, Middlesex, England

First published in this edition by Hamish Hamilton 1992
Published in Puffin Books 1994
1 3 5 7 9 10 8 6 4 2

Printed in England by Clays Ltd, St Ives plc
Filmset in Baskerville

Contents

Contents

Chapter One

A Blooming Parcel

From the depths of the cave called Dragon's Tooth came a roar so mighty that the ground shook, sending clumps of sandy soil tumbling down the steep sides of Silverton Combe. Drivers leaned out of their cars to see if a low-flying jet had passed overhead, rabbits emerged from their burrows with the speed of champagne corks and startled birds left their trees for the safety of the sky.

In the village of Silverton, just below the caves, cups and saucers trembled on their shelves and the landlord of the 'George and Dragon' apologised to his wife for his indigestion, which had been troubling him, he said, since lunchtime. It was then six o'clock.

It was all over in a few seconds. Some earth movement deep in the network of limestone caves beneath Mendip, suggested the experts.

Most likely the crumbling walls of an underground tunnel had at last collapsed.

Local people shook their heads wisely and said no, it was more likely to have been the dragon.

Simon Peter Richard Ogden, known to his friends as Sprog, was not in the best of spirits. He stood leaning against a post outside Bath station, thoughtfully kicking a wire litter-bin.

'Don't do that, dear,' said the lady from Aunts Anonymous, an agency which provided escorts for children travelling alone. She was not in the best of spirits either since they had already been

waiting an hour. 'I wonder where your aunt can be!' she said for the third time.

Sprog scowled. 'She's probably so absent-minded she's forgotten I'm coming.' He had never met his Great Aunt Cissie Stokes, but he had heard about her. 'Bit of an old witch,' his father said once when they received a Christmas card from her on June 4th, 'and nutty as a fruitcake!'

That was before there had been any question of having to spend the Easter holidays with her. Now suddenly, as far as his parents were concerned, the nutty old witch had turned into a sweet, reliable old lady. 'You'll be much better off with her,' his mother had written on the flimsy airmail paper. 'Things are turning rather nasty out here at the moment. There's a strict curfew at night and the airport has been closed for a week. Your father and I shall feel much happier knowing you're safely down in Somerset with Aunt Cis. Don't think you're missing anything out here. Francis and Meg are getting fed up with having to stay indoors all the time.'

Francis and Meg were only little, too young to be sent away to boarding school. But not too young, it seemed, to be where the action was. It was only because Sprog had grown too old for the local English-speaking school that his parents were forced to send him to be educated in England.

'Packed me off like a parcel, they have,' he muttered. 'A blooming parcel!'

At the sound of a shot both he and the Anonymous Aunt jumped visibly. An ancient car, backfiring, had drawn up to the kerb. Out of it climbed an equally ancient man, with a thatch of grey hair and a straggly grey moustache, wearing a strange coat covered with different coloured patches and fringed at the bottom like a lampshade.

He came towards them and bowed gallantly.

'Excuse me, ma'am, but would this young gentleman be the great-nephew of Miss Cissie Stokes, by any chance?'

'Yes, he would,' said the Aunt faintly. 'And you are—?'

'Talker Harris, at your service.' He gave another bow, even more gallant than the first. 'I am Miss Stokes's chauffeur.'

The Aunt mopped her forehead with a handkerchief. 'You're very late, Mr. Harris.'

'It was the car,' he explained. 'Temperamental old girl, she is.'

Sprog went to take a closer look. 'What is it?' he called.

'She's a Morris Oxford.' Talker's chest

swelled with pride. 'Miss Stokes has owned that car since 1956.'

Sprog threw his cases into the back and settled down in the passenger seat. 'Come on, then. Let's go.'

'Right, sir!' Talker turned courteously to the Aunt. He bowed for the third time, the fringe of his coat sweeping the ground, and climbed into the driving seat.

After a few false starts the Morris burst into life and moved jerkily away from the kerb. At the last moment Sprog remembered to turn and wave to the Anonymous Aunt, who waved back before wearily retracing her steps into the station.

Only those with nerves of steel could have enjoyed being driven through the late evening traffic by Talker Harris, but fortunately Sprog was so blessed. Once they were out of the city and onto the open road his spirits began to lift a little.

'This is a fantastic car, Mr . . . ?'

'Harris. But most people call me Talker. Because I am one, you see. It's the thing I'm best at. Spinning a yarn, Miss Cis calls it.'

'Talker, what's Aunt Cis like? Is she very old?'

Talker scratched his head, causing the Morris to swerve from the left side of the road to the right and back again, just in time to miss an oncoming car. 'Pretty old, I'd say. If she's your father's aunt she must be pretty old, mustn't she? Oh yes, she's pretty old.' He racked his brains even further. 'And she has a cat.'

Sprog's heart sank. All witches had cats. 'Have you known her long?'

Again Talker scratched his head and again the car swerved. 'Must be about thirty years now. Ever since I used to drive trucks for her brother when he had the transport business. That was me job, you see – doing long hauls. But then old Mr. Stokes died and the firm moved to Bristol, so Miss Cis, she lets me have this loft over the barn to keep me clobber in and in return I does a few jobs for her. Every now and again I gets a bit restless and takes off for a while and then I comes back and has a rest. A travelling man I am, by nature.'

By now Sprog was only listening with half his mind, because the other half was occupied with the state of his stomach. Visions of steak and chips kept flashing before his eyes. Or sausages and baked beans and chips. Or fried chicken with sweetcorn and chips. But stew from a witch's cauldron – no, thank you very much!

'Do you know this part of the world at all?' inquired Talker.

'No, I've never been here before.'

'Takes a bit of knowing. They're a fine range of hills, the Mendips. But mysterious – very mysterious.' He slid his eyes round to see if he had captured his audience.

'In what way mysterious?' asked Sprog, who had by now mentally reached the jelly-and-ice-cream stage.

'Caves. Right deep in the earth. Caves and underground rivers and tunnels. You've heard of Cheddar Gorge and Wookey Hole?'

'Oh yes, I've heard of them. But I didn't know they were anywhere near here.'

'Well, they've been discovered a lot now and made electric so you can see everything, which sort of destroys the mystery, if you know what I mean. But we've got caves in Silverton and they're still as dark as the middle of the earth, which is where they go down to, I daresay. There's a dragon lives in one of them.'

'A dragon?' Sprog repeated, not believing his ears.

Talker nodded. 'They call it the Dragon's Tooth Cave, on account of the dragon having left one of its molars lying around in there, and if you go to Silverton museum you can see it, large as life and twenty times larger than any tooth you and me have got in our heads. Anyways, he roars a bit now and again, just to remind us he's still around.'

Sprog only just managed to stop himself laughing aloud.

'Matter of fact,' Talker went on, 'he did a bit of roaring today and the ground shook so much that everything went jigging about on the shelves and a bottle of elderberry wine fell off the dresser in your aunt's kitchen and smashed on the floor. The cat lapped it up and now she's sprawled out on the sofa, dead drunk, and serve her right!'

'Fancy that,' said Sprog.

'You don't believe me, do you?'

'I'm a little old for dragon stories,' Sprog pointed out tactfully.

'Well, I'm not,' said Talker. 'And you wouldn't catch me poking around them caves, I can tell you!'

On and on they drove, at the same erratic pace, along roads where they met less and less traffic and passed only the occasional house. Sprog began to feel depressed again. Like a lamb to the slaughter, he thought, he was being taken to spend the holidays with a witch, a mad old tinker and a drunken cat!

Now they were driving up a hill between steep wooded banks. 'This is Silverton Combe,' said Talker. He slowed down the car. 'I don't suppose you can see that dark hole over there? That's what we calls a swallet. Goes deep into the earth, it does. Folk throw coins in there and never hear them fall.'

Sprog stifled a yawn. He had almost passed the hunger stage by now. A glass of milk and bed was all he wanted.

Talker noticed the yawn. 'Not much further to go,' he promised.

At the top of the hill they turned left into a narrow lane which kept curving round until Sprog felt sure they must be going in a complete circle. Suddenly the Morris came to a standstill as the engine coughed and died.

'This is it,' said Talker. 'Dolphin Cottage. And there's your aunt, waiting to welcome you.'

Dimly silhouetted against a narrow ray of light from the hallway stood the towering figure of an elderly woman, holding aloft a lantern which lit up her curved beak of a nose. Around her legs rubbed a strange, primrose-coloured cat.

Weary and hopeless, Sprog trudged up the path.

Chapter Two

The Cave

When the morning sunlight fell on his pillow Sprog thought he was in his bed at school and waited for the bell to jerk him awake. Then his hand encountered a wall where there was not usually a wall and he sat up with a start. Of course! He was in Aunt Cissie Stokes's cottage at Silverton.

And Aunt Cis? Well, she was not quite what he had expected. For one thing she was as tall as his father, not at all the wrinkled old lady he had imagined. Her greeting had been matter-of-fact, but friendly. 'Do we call you Simon or Peter or Richard?' she had asked.

'I'm usually called Sprog.'

'Fair enough. And how hungry are you, Sprog?'

'Pretty hungry.' He had eyed the kitchen

range suspiciously. Heaven only knew what she might be brewing up on that!

'How about some soup, followed by chicken pie? That suit you too, Talker?'

'Suit us both, I shouldn't wonder,' said Talker, winking at Sprog.

And it had suited him, very well. In fact his appetite had returned with a rush. What's more, he was still alive this morning.

In the light of day he decided he did not really believe in witches any more than he believed in dragons. He jumped out of bed, washed sketchily, and dressed in jeans and a sweat-shirt.

Aunt Cis glanced up when he entered the kitchen. 'Good morning, Sprog. Fancy some eggs and bacon?'

'Yes, please!'

'Carry on, then. Frying pan's on the shelf over your head and there's some fat in the fridge.'

Sprog dug his hands into his pockets. 'I don't think I'll bother.'

'Never cooked your own breakfast before?' inquired Aunt Cis without surprise. 'Well, now's the time to start. I'll show you how.'

It was easier than he had imagined. True, the sausage ended up black on one side and the egg broke when he took it out of the pan, but it tasted all right. All the better, in fact, for being his own work. 'That wasn't bad,' he remarked, feeling pleased with himself as he pushed his plate aside to make room for brown bread and honey.

Aunt Cis sat down to share a pot of tea with him. 'Anyone can cook if they've a mind to. There's no mystery in it, though some like to pretend there is.'

Sprog studied his great aunt with interest. She was not really at all frightening, despite her curved nose, which this morning looked rather noble, like Julius Caesar's. Her face was long and her eyes were grey, clear and direct. She was dressed in a large overall shaped like a tent, and brown corduroy trousers.

She bent down to stroke the cat as it pressed against her legs, nose alert to the smell of food. 'It's your bacon she's after.'

'Shall I give her my rind?'

'If you like.'

Sprog cut up the rind and offered a piece to the cat.

'What's her name?'

'So-So.'

The cat took the rind with great delicacy and retired beneath the table to eat it.

'She's decided to give me a chance,' said Sprog. 'Later on she might even accept me.'

Aunt Cis said approvingly, 'Good! I'm glad

you're the sort of boy who understands animals. Did you bring your wellingtons with you?' He nodded. 'Then when you've finished breakfast we'll collect the torch and I'll show you the kind of places you can explore.'

'Why do we need a torch?' asked Sprog, thinking it rather odd considering it was broad daylight.

'To see in the dark, of course.'

'In the dark of a cave?' he asked hopefully.

'Where else?'

'Oh, great!'

As they walked up the lane Sprog noticed a dark hole in the ground surrounded by boulders and almost masked by undergrowth. 'I know what that is,' he said. 'It's a swallet. Talker told me about them last night.'

'That's right. It's really a hole where a stream has gone underground. You'll find this interesting countryside to explore provided you look where you're going.'

The thought of tripping unawares down a swallet made Sprog go cold. You could lie around at the bottom of one until you were nothing but skin and bone and then just bone and no one would guess what had become of you . . .

'But you look a sensible sort of boy,' Aunt Cis was saying, 'so I daresay you'll come to no harm. These are called Silverton Woods and this path leads to Tibor Rocks, where the caves begin.'

'Are we going to the dragon's cave – the one where the tooth was found?'

'We can, if you like.'

As they reached the rocks the weather, which up to that moment had been fair, took a change for the worse. A sudden gusty wind blew up and the clouds drew together menacingly overhead. 'Let's hurry,' said Aunt Cis, as they felt the first splashes of rain on their faces.

They passed other openings on their way up the hillside, nearly all of them low or narrow, so Sprog was surprised when they stopped outside a fairly large entrance. 'This is it,' said Aunt Cis. 'And only just in time!' As she spoke the rain came sheeting down and they dashed for the opening.

After a few yards Aunt Cis switched on her powerful torch to illumine a long, high chamber.

'I can hear water,' said Sprog.

'Drip-dripping all the time,' said Aunt Cis. 'Shall we go in a bit farther?'

He moved forward gingerly, sliding his feet over the uneven floor of the cave in case a sudden gap should open up in front of him. 'Where was the tooth found?' he asked, his voice echoing around the lofty chamber.

'Just about there.' Aunt Cis shone her torch over a flattish area strewn with small boulders.

Suddenly Sprog realised why the floor at the far end of the cave seemed so much blacker than the rest. 'It's a pool of water!' he exclaimed. 'How deep is it?'

'Very deep, according to the cave divers. There's a hole at one side leading into quite a long tunnel – they call it a sump when it's underwater. It leads into another large chamber and then another, getting smaller all the time.'

'You mean the cave divers actually go down into that water and swim through the tunnels in the dark?'

'They have the right equipment, of course, like miners. They've explored pretty well every inch of these caves – and made maps of them.'

'Can I borrow the torch and come up here by myself sometimes?'

'Not by yourself,' said Aunt Cis. 'That's an unwise thing to do. Always explore in pairs, at least. Did you notice that large modern house next-door-but-one to Dolphin Cottage? Well, there's a family called Spruce who've just come to live there. Father's a dentist in Bristol.'

Sprog pulled a face. He hated all dentists as a

matter of principle.

'There are three children,' Aunt Cis went on. 'I should think the boy, Jonathan, is about your age. He might like to come exploring with you. Or else you could bring Talker and leave him outside the cave. He won't come in because he's scared, especially of this particular cave, but if you should get into difficulties then he'd be within earshot.'

'Why is he scared? Because of the dragon?'

'Partly. And partly because this one is supposed to be haunted by the ghost of a hermit who lived here in the sixteenth century.'

'A dragon *and* a ghost, all in one cave!' exclaimed Sprog. He shot a quick look at Aunt Cis. 'Do you believe in them?'

'I'm always careful about saying I *dis*believe anything,' she said. 'That seems to me a rather dangerous, dead-end sort of line to take. Let's just say I've never personally seen either of them.'

'But you've seen the tooth?'

'Oh, yes – and you can see it too if you visit our local museum.'

Sprog looked into the inky blackness of the water. What secrets did it hold? The thought of that tunnel beneath the water both scared and fascinated him at the same time.

'You have the torch for a while,' Aunt Cis suggested, 'while I go outside to see if it's stopped raining.'

Left alone in the cave, listening to the monotonous drip-drip of the water, he felt suddenly sad and lonely. He thought of his mother and father, of Meg, Francis, heat, flies and curfew, and wished he could be with them all, far away from this icy, dank darkness.

Then he heard it.

A long deep sigh.

He flashed the torch around the cave and saw shapes that shifted and wavered in the beam of light. 'Shadows,' he murmured to himself. 'Only shadows.' He was getting as bad as Talker, except that he was not afraid. No, strangely enough, he was not afraid. He was conscious, though, of pain in his jaw and put his hand over his mouth.

'Seen any dragons?' His great aunt's voice came from behind him, making him jump.

'I did hear something,' he said slowly. 'A low moaning sound . . .'

'Most likely the wind down a swallet,' said Aunt Cis. 'It can make odd noises.'

He shook his head. 'This was more like a sigh.'

'The rain's almost stopped,' said Aunt Cis. 'I think we'd better get back before it starts again.'

Reluctantly he followed her out of the cave, switching off the torch as they reached daylight.

'What's the matter with your face?' inquired Aunt Cis.

Only then did he realise he was still holding his hand over his mouth. Toothache! It had suddenly come on in the cave. Having no wish to be whisked off to the dentist, especially as there was one living next-door-but-one, he took his hand away hastily. 'Nothing,' he said. 'Nothing at all.'

'Sure?' she persisted.

'Quite sure,' he said.

She took the hint and led the way down the hillside towards the woods.

Once out in the open air Sprog began to feel better and the home-sickness which had swept over him in the cave receded. Even his toothache disappeared. It had been only a twinge, after all.

As for the sigh, it seemed to him more and more likely to have been the wind. Just the wind down a swallet.

Chapter Three

The Spruce Family

The next day was Sunday and Sprog accompanied Aunt Cis to Silverton parish church. As soon as they were settled in a pew she pointed out the Spruce family, on the other side of the aisle. 'I'll introduce you to them after the service,' she said, and then to his surprise suddenly disappeared in the direction of the vestry.

He studied the Spruces with interest. Mr. Spruce looked large and prosperous with a self-important air, but all Sprog could see of Mrs. Spruce was a longish nose and a few wisps of wiry gold hair. The rest of her face was hidden beneath the curved brim of a navy-blue hat.

As for the children, they looked unbelievably neat and well-scrubbed. All three had fair hair, the boy's cut very short to reveal his pale pink neck, while the eldest girl wore hers long and kept flicking her head so that it swung like a curtain. Only the youngest girl looked as though she did not fit into the family mould. Her hair was short and curly and she fidgeted in her seat, whereas her brother and sister sat bolt upright like their parents.

Sprog, however, paid them no further attention once he realised it was Aunt Cis playing the organ. He could see little of her except her head bobbing up and down behind the choir stalls, but the hymns certainly went with a swing.

'You played well,' he told her when they met outside afterwards. 'Good and loud.'

'Thanks,' she said, before striding off down the path to intercept Mrs. Spruce, who was making a regal exit from the church followed by her husband and the three meek-looking children.

'I'd like to introduce my great-nephew, Simon Ogden,' Aunt Cis began. 'He's staying with me during the school holidays.'

'How d'you do,' said Mrs. Spruce in a bored voice. She put out a limp hand for Sprog to shake. 'And where do you go to school?'

Sprog told her and her expression grew a shade warmer. 'How extraordinary. I have a nephew there. Philip Pond. Do you know him?'

Sprog knew him all right. They called him

Weedy Pond and he was famous for stealing other people's biscuits. 'Yes, I know him,' he said non-committally.

'Isn't that amazing?' Mrs. Spruce bent backwards like a reed in the wind to speak to her husband. 'Christopher, this boy knows Philip. Isn't that an amazing coincidence?'

'Amazing,' echoed Mr. Spruce.

'You must come and play with Jonathan.' Mrs. Spruce turned to her son, who was making patterns in the gravel with his foot. 'Don't scuff your shoes, dear. You'll ruin them.'

Jonathan scowled ferociously.

She gave Aunt Cis a gracious nod and said, 'I'll telephone you, Miss Stokes,' before leading her family down the path.

Sprog watched them go. 'He didn't look too friendly.'

'Probably shy,' Aunt Cis said charitably.

While she prepared the Sunday dinner – roast lamb with sprigs of rosemary from the garden – Sprog sat down with his pad of airmail paper to write a letter to his parents.

Composition did not come easily to him. The beginning was all right – 'Dear Mum and Dad, I hope you are well and not dying of the heat' – but when he came to telling them about Silverton and Aunt Cis words seemed to fail him. He sat chewing the top of his pen for a while and then he wrote, 'Aunt Cis is very . . .' He had been going to say 'nice', but somehow that was not quite the right word for Aunt Cis, so he changed it to 'well'. 'I like Dolphin Cottage,' he added. A flash of inspiration came to him. 'There are a lot of caves round here.' But that sounded as if the caves were somehow mixed up with the cottage, so he finished off hastily, 'I am quite well but I would rather be with you. I wouldn't mind the danger. Love, Sprog.'

In the afternoon, when he had recovered from the effects of an enormous Sunday dinner, he took the letter up to the village and posted it. On the way back, passing the Spruces' square, modern house, he heard a faint cry of 'Help!' and stood still, wondering if he had imagined it. But no, there it was again, coming from the direction of a shed at the side of the house. 'Help! Please help!'

Sprog looked around uncertainly and saw there was no one else in sight. Feeling somewhat apprehensive he walked up the drive and peered through the window into the shed. The tear-stained face of the youngest Spruce girl stared back at him. She must have shut herself in. He tried the door handle and found it stuck fast, but after a few seconds of determined tugging it suddenly opened, sending Sprog crashing back on to the path.

'Oh, thank you!' The small girl rushed out to help him back on his feet. 'I thought I was stuck in there for ever and ever and no one would find me until I was dead.' She burst into noisy sobs. 'And they wouldn't even *care*!'

Sprog guessed she was about six years old, the same age as his sister Meg, who was also very good at turning on the tap when she wanted sympathy. 'Where's the rest of your family?' he inquired, thinking that if Jonathan were around somewhere he might be able to fix up a joint expedition to the caves.

'Daddy's asleep, Mummy and Caroline have gone out to tea with friends and Jonathan's doing his stamps up in his room. Nobody cares what happens to me.' She sniffed and wiped the tears away with the back of her hand. 'Have you got a handkerchief?'

He had, but it was not respectable enough to offer. 'Why don't you use your skirt?' he suggested.

'I couldn't do that! Oh, look . . .' Horrified, she stared down at her blue-and-white cotton dress. 'I've got a mark on it. Mummy will be *furious*. It's this dirty old shed.'

'What were you doing in there, anyway?'

'Playing houses. I was having a tea party, with real tea and doughnuts.' Her round face brightened. 'Would you like a doughnut? It's got oodles of jam inside. I added some more out of the jar when Mummy wasn't looking.'

Sprog hesitated. He was particularly fond of doughnuts and even though he had just eaten a large meal he felt pretty sure he could manage one. 'All right,' he said cautiously.

She led him into the hut and presented him with a sugary doughnut oozing strawberry jam from every side. 'My name's Charlotte,' she said. 'My sister's called Caroline and my brother's name is Jonathan. What's yours?'

'Sprog.' He stared down at the doughnut, wondering how best to tackle it.

'That's not a real name.'

'No, it's my nickname.' He decided to begin by licking off the excess jam. 'If you were my sister I'd probably call you Charley for short.'

'Mummy doesn't like our names to be shortened. She gets furious if Jonathan calls me Charley—'

'I can't think why,' said a voice from the doorway. 'Because that's what she is – a right Charley.'

Sprog swung round to see Jonathan Spruce propped against the doorway, his arms folded and an unfriendly expression on his face.

'And just what do you think you're doing in our shed?' Jonathan demanded. 'I suppose you realise you're trespassing.'

'He came to help me,' Charley said quickly. 'I got shut in and screamed and screamed, but you didn't hear me because you were too busy with your silly old stamps. His name's Sprog.' She beamed at her rescuer.

Jonathan laughed. 'Sprog!' He laughed again and repeated unbelievingly, 'Sprog! That's just the sort of stupid name a boy who goes to boarding school would have.'

Sprog flushed. 'It's not my fault I go to a boarding school,' he said. 'My parents have to live abroad because of my dad's job, but when they come back I shall live at home again.'

'Mummy and Daddy wouldn't send any of us away to boarding school,' said Charlotte, unexpectedly siding with her brother. 'They like us too much.'

'My parents like me too,' Sprog protested. 'They didn't want to send me away.'

'I'll bet they did!' Jonathan jeered. 'Like Philip's mum and dad. They couldn't wait to get rid of him. No wonder you've ended up at the same stupid school.' His grin turned into a threatening frown. 'You'd better beat it – and don't ever let me catch you in our garden again!'

Sprog, trying to look unconcerned, edged his way out of the shed, but at the last moment Jonathan put out a foot to trip him up. Sprog stumbled and fell headlong through the open door, landing heavily on the path for the second time that afternoon and sending the remains of his doughnut flying into the herbaceous border.

'Okay, get lost!' said Jonathan, towering over him.

Sprog saw red. He got to his feet slowly, pretending to dust himself down, then wheeled around and butted Jonathan in the stomach. Taken by surprise, Jonathan fell back into the shed, narrowly missing Charley, who gave a shriek of delight. 'That was good!' she told Sprog approvingly. 'Now hit him some more.'

Sprog glanced down at Jonathan, who was lying winded on the floor, and shook his head. 'Too easy. Cheers! It's been nice knowing you.'

He whistled cheerfully as he made his way back to Dolphin Cottage. He hadn't had so much satisfaction from a scuffle since his last encounter with Weedy Pond. Although, to tell the truth, he felt rather sorry for poor old Weedy if what Jonathan said was true about his parents wanting to get rid of him.

As he arrived at the gate of Dolphin Cottage

he wiped his nose on his hand and found that it was bloody, so he went round to the back door, hoping to sneak in and clean up before Aunt Cis saw him.

As luck would have it she was in the kitchen baking a cake. She glanced up when he entered and raised her eyebrows inquiringly. 'I hadn't realised going to the Post Office could be that dangerous?'

He grinned. 'I met Jonathan Spruce.'

'Ah!' said Aunt Cis. 'Who won?'

'I did.'

'That's good. A pity, though, he's turned out not to be friendly. It looks as if you'll have to take Talker exploring with you tomorrow after all.'

Sprog nodded, thinking he didn't mind too much about Jonathan Spruce. He would rather explore the cave by himself, anyway. There was something special about it he didn't particularly want to share with anyone else.

Chapter Four

Exploring

'Where's Talker?' Sprog asked next morning when he came into the kitchen for breakfast.

'Still in bed,' Aunt Cis replied. 'Why don't you take over this mug of tea and wake him up.'

Sprog carried the mug carefully out of the back door and into the side entrance of the barn, where the Morris was kept. He mounted the steep, rickety steps that led up to the hayloft, precariously balancing the tea in one hand, and emerged into a large shadowy space cluttered with old tea-chests and shabby furniture. At first he could not see Talker at all, but eventually realised that what he thought was a pile of old rugs in the corner was in fact covering a bed, and under the rugs was a hump that could be a human shape.

He approached the bed and said, 'Talker? I've brought you some tea.'

'Whassat?' Talker's unshaven face appeared over the rugs. He yawned and blinked his eyes several times in an effort to get them open. 'What time is it?'

'Getting on,' said Sprog.

Talker took the mug and drained the tea in one gulp. 'Didn't bring a biscuit as well, by any chance?'

'No, but I'll make your breakfast if you're ready to get up.'

Talker gave him a puzzled look. 'Would there be something happening today I've forgotten about?'

'It's a fine morning.' Sprog pulled back the checked tea-cloth hanging on a piece of wire over the window. 'I thought I might go for a walk.'

'U-uh,' said Talker warily.

'The trouble is,' Sprog went on, 'I want to go and look at the caves but Aunt Cis says I can't go on my own, so I thought you might like to come with me?'

Talker looked far from enthusiastic. 'Up to them caves?'

'Aunt Cis says it doesn't matter if you stay outside. It's just that she thinks someone ought to be around in case I fall down a hole or something. Not that I'm likely to, but you know how women fuss.'

'Women, yes,' Talker agreed, 'but your Aunt Cis is a different kettle of fish. If she says someone ought to be around, then someone ought. But – ahem!' He paused to give a dramatic cough. 'You see, I have this spot of bother with me chest. Can't stand the damp – it plays havoc with me bronchials. So I have to keep out of caves, you see, for medical reasons.'

'I quite understand,' Sprog assured him. 'In fact, I'd rather explore by myself.'

'Blowed if I would!' Talker handed him back the empty mug. 'Now if you like to start that bacon sizzling in the pan I'll be there directly.'

After breakfast they climbed up to Tibor Rocks, but when Sprog made straight for the entrance to the Dragon's Tooth cave, Talker turned several shades paler than his normal weather-beaten rust colour.

'Hey, you can't go in there,' he said anxiously. 'Strange things go on in that cave – noises, for instance.'

'I've heard them. It's only the wind.'

'Wind, my foot! That's spooks – the ghost of this old hermit what used to live in there hundreds of years ago. They found his bones lying around on a shelf—'

'I know,' Sprog interrupted impatiently.

'Aunt Cis told me about him, but I still want to go in. Just wait out here for me. I promise I won't be long.'

Grumbling, Talker sat down on a boulder and took out his pipe. 'I don't like it,' he muttered. 'And ten to one the dragon won't like it either.'

Sprog stood for a moment, studying the cave entrance.

It looked very black and the ground around it was surprisingly bare of vegetation. He switched on the torch and advanced slowly into the entrance.

On either side he saw strange rock formations and suspended above him a curtain of stalactites. The farther he went in the colder it became. He stopped and flashed the torchbeam up to the ceiling to see how high it was. Probably about seven metres.

At last he saw the shimmer of water and knew he was near the pool. He moved the light down the walls to the pool, which appeared to shelve gradually, like a beach. If only there were another way into the next chamber, through a tunnel, but not underwater. Then he could really explore!

So far, at least, there had been no noises, but perhaps they only occurred when the wind was blowing from a certain direction. The odd thing was that he had toothache again, as he had on the first visit to the cave. He supposed it must have something to do with the damp.

Cautiously he sat down on a boulder close to the pool. Wondering how deep it was he directed the torchbeam into the blackness. It would not look black in daylight, of course; more of a muddy brown. The circle of light was reflected back at him. No, there were three circles of light . . .

He moved the torch. Only one circle followed. The other two stayed where they were. He glanced up at the roof. No light coming in from there. Could there be underwater lamps fixed up by the cave divers?

But these seemed to be resting on top of the water. As he watched they both disappeared for a moment and then reappeared. As if someone – or something – had blinked.

Strangely enough, he was not scared. He felt that odd sadness, as he had last time, and he felt toothache. His heart was beating fast but it was mostly excitement. Was he about to see Talker's dragon at last?

With his eyes fixed on those two circles of light he groped behind him for a loose stone or something to throw into the pool and disturb

whatever it was that glared at him so intently.

Suddenly the waters began to move and in the light from his torch Sprog saw a head appear. He was so surprised he nearly fell off the boulder, but could not tear his gaze away from the thing rising up in the centre of the pool. It was like no creature he had ever seen before, in some ways resembling a dragon's head but with a strange helmet on top. His hand found a piece of rock that had broken off from the side, about the size of a shoe.

Then he heard it again. The deep sighing sound.

Chapter Five

Minerva

'Don't do that. Please don't do that!'

Sprog raised the stone above his head.

'I don't mean you any harm. Please don't throw that stone.'

He stared unbelievingly at the creature. 'Are you a dragon?' he asked.

'What's a dragon?' The mournful eyes gazed at him.

'Well, it's a—' Sprog searched for the right words. 'I don't know really, but you do look very much like one. At least – er, how much more of you is there underneath the water?'

The creature glanced down. 'Quite a lot.'

'Can you breathe fire?'

'I'm not sure. I've never tried. To be honest, I don't really feel like trying, not just now. I haven't been at all well lately.'

'I'm sorry to hear that,' said Sprog politely. 'I hope it's nothing serious?'

'The most frightful toothache. I've hardly been able to get any sleep at all. Can you see anything?' It opened its mouth wide, revealing a hideous array of teeth. Sprog shrank back against the cave wall. 'It's somewhere around the left-hand side at the bottom, towards the back.'

Sprog took a firm hold on the torch and shone it along the rows and rows of teeth. 'They look all right to me,' he said. 'But you've an awful lot of them, haven't you?'

'A couple of thousand, actually, give or take a few. I lose one from time to time, but they grow again.'

Sprog nodded. 'I think there's one in Silverton museum. Anyway I'm not surprised you've got toothache. I've had it both times I've been in this cave. I think it's the damp.'

'No, that's probably *my* toothache you can feel. You're a very sympathetic person, you know. In fact, you're the only living creature I've been able to talk to since I last saw my husband. He left the cave to go and fight the Tyrant King some while ago and hasn't come back. I'm afraid—' The creature stopped. Two enormous tears welled up in her eyes and ran down to splash into the water. Sprog offered her his handkerchief and out of the water came a surprisingly short, skinny arm. She took the handkerchief in her claw and dabbed her eyes before returning it to Sprog. 'Thank you. I'm so sorry. I get rather upset when I think of him. He was such a fine, gentle person and so brave. The Tyrant King had trapped us in this cave and we were so dreadfully hungry that at last my husband said he must go out to find food. I begged him not to go, but he wouldn't listen to me. 'Stay here,' he said, 'and don't come out until I tell you it's safe.' And I've been waiting ever since.'

'But who's the Tyrant King?' asked Sprog. The named tugged at his memory, but he could not remember where he had heard it before.

'Oh, a fearsome beast! As tall as this cave and with a *very* unpleasant temper. You must take care . . .'

'He's nowhere around now,' Sprog assured her. 'But how is it nobody's ever found you? Do you live down there, at the bottom of the pool?'

'My goodness, no. I've a comfortable, dry little cave just along the tunnel that leads out of this pool.'

'My Aunt Cis says all these caves have been explored. People have swum along that tunnel.'

43

'Not along *my* tunnel. You must mean the other one, higher up. I've seen people swimming along there. They've never found mine, I don't know why.'

'But how have you managed for food, if you haven't been out of the cave?'

'It hasn't been easy. I grew very thin – that's how I managed to get through to my cave. I eat only occasionally, whatever I can find just outside the entrance, and I sleep a good deal – that helps to pass the time. The only contact I've had with anyone apart from yourself was with Hugh the Hermit. Such a nice man! He talked to me a good deal, but he couldn't understand me nearly as well as you do.'

Sprog tried to remember what Aunt Cis had told him about the hermit who once lived in the cave. Sixteenth century – he was almost certain she had said it was during the sixteenth century.

'He gave me a name, too,' the creature went on. 'He called me Minerva – after some foreign goddess, I believe.'

'I know!' Sprog exclaimed, thinking back to his Ancient History book. On the cover was the statue of Athena, the Greek goddess, wearing her helmet, just like the creature in front of him. And Minerva was the Roman name for Athena! A hermit living in the sixteenth century would probably read and write in Latin – naturally he would call her Minerva. 'It suits you exactly,' he told her.

'Do you like it? You will call me by it, won't you? No one has since Hugh went. Do *you* have a name?'

'I've four. Simon Peter Richard Ogden. But you can call me Sprog.'

'Sprog,' she repeated slowly. 'I like that – oh, Sprog, I'm so glad you've come! It's wonderful to have a normal conversation again after all this time. Hugh kept making noises, as if that would help me understand him, poor fellow.'

Sprog stared at her in amazement. For the

first time it occurred to him that he had not uttered a single word. Nor had he heard her voice, except in his mind . . .

'You hadn't realised!' Minerva exclaimed. 'Do all humans, then, speak with noises?'

'Yes,' said Sprog wonderingly. 'Yes, they do. But what we're doing is . . . *thinking* our conversation! That's why I picked up your toothache the first time I came into the cave, and your sadness . . . Minerva.'

'Oh, that's so nice,' she breathed. 'Say it again.'

'Minerva,' he repeated. 'I believe you're real, aren't you? I don't mean to sound rude, but I don't think you can be a dragon, because they only exist in people's minds.'

'Oh, people are always on about dragons!' she complained. 'Hugh talked about dragons. And quite a while before Hugh there were all these young men who kept coming into my cave waving swords and yelling things about dragons . . .'

'That was probably St. George and some other knights,' said Sprog. 'In those days they used to look for dragons so they could rescue ladies in distress.'

'In that case they should have recognised me as a lady in distress and not a dragon! Then they might have tried to help me instead of frightening the life out of me.'

'But if you're *not* a dragon,' Sprog went on, 'the only other thing you could be is a dinosaur and that's impossible because they're extinct. Unless . . .'

He looked thoughtfully at Minerva's strange head, with its crested helmet and a nose that flattened out like a duck's bill.

'Unless what?' she prompted.

'Unless you're the only one left. The only one to survive.'

Minerva's enormous mouth quivered a little. She opened her eyes wide. 'The only one?' she repeated faintly.

Sprog clapped his hand to his forehead. 'Of course! Tyrannosaurus Rex – the Tyrant King!' he exclaimed. 'Then *you* must be one of the duck-billed dinosaurs.'

'What do you mean – the only one?' she persisted.

'No dinosaurs have lived on earth for millions of years. Since before the Ice Age, in fact.'

'It did get very cold at one time, but I stayed in the cave and went to sleep.'

Sprog said sadly, 'I'm afraid you probably *are* the only dinosaur left. If anyone else had found one there'd have been a fuss about it, like the

Loch Ness monster.'

At that moment they became aware of shouting outside the cave. 'Hey! Hey there, young
Sprog! Are you all right?'

'That's Talker,' Sprog told her. He shouted in
the direction of the cave opening, 'I'm okay. Just
coming . . .'

Minerva sighed. 'Must you go?'

'I'll be back, I promise. And I'll try to bring
you something for the toothache. Though I don't
suppose aspirin will have much effect on you,
being so – well, larger than the average person.'
A sudden idea struck him. 'Minerva, did you let
out a loud roar recently?'

'I may have done, dear boy,' she said vaguely.

'You made the whole hillside tremble. They
thought it was an earthquake.'

'I'm most awfully sorry. Please do apologise
for me.'

'I will. At least . . .' He could hear Talker
calling again. 'I must go. I'll be back later.'

As he reached the opening he heard Minerva's
mournful, 'Goodbye, Sprog. Don't forget . . .'

Chapter Six

Silverton Museum

'Well?' Talker inquired. 'Did you see the dragon?'

Sprog hesitated. If he told Talker the truth, by this afternoon the cave would be crowded with people looking for Minerva and sending divers down to find the other tunnel.

Unless, of course, he made sure no one would believe Talker.

'Did you?' prompted Talker.

'Oh, yes. I saw the dragon. I even talked to it.'

'Pull the other leg,' Talker growled. 'Anything else?'

'What more do you want?'

'The ghost? Did you see anything spooky?'

'You mean the hermit? No, I didn't see him. Only the dragon.'

Talker gave a loud sniff. 'All the same, sooner

I get away from this place the happier I shall be!' He set off at a shambling pace down the hillside.

Sprog cast a final look into the cave. 'I'll be back,' he said silently, directing his thoughts to Minerva. Then he ran down the hill, quickly overtaking Talker.

When he reached Dolphin Cottage Aunt Cis was in the back garden, digging in the vegetable patch. Watching her over the fence was an old shire horse. Sprog went up to stroke his broad, dappled-grey nose.

'His name's Samson,' said Aunt Cis, glancing up. 'When Mr. Priddy gave up farming and came to live next door he couldn't bring himself to sell Samson, so now they're both enjoying an honourable retirement.'

Into Sprog's mind came a picture of Samson's past life as one of the finest pairs of heavy horses in the county. 'Aunt Cis,' he said slowly, 'do you think it's possible for some people to talk to animals through their thoughts. I mean, have an actual conversation with them?'

Aunt Cis picked up the fork and began walking up the path towards the house. 'It would have to be a rare human being. One in a million million, I'd say. But anything's possible.'

Would Aunt Cis consider a living dinosaur possible? wondered Sprog as he followed her. He was tempted to tell her about Minerva, but decided against it. It was not that he was afraid she would tell everyone, like Talker, but he wanted Minerva to be his secret for a while longer.

'Did you enjoy the caves?' asked Aunt Cis as she leant her fork against the wall and opened the back door.

'Brilliant!' He waited while she took off her boots and then followed her into the kitchen. 'Aunt Cis, do you know a cure for toothache? Apart from aspirin, I mean?'

She gave him a sharp look. 'Why? Are you having trouble?'

'No, not me,' he said hastily. 'Just a friend. Someone I met this morning.'

'The only real cure is to go to the dentist.'

'It's not bad enough for that. Isn't there anything else?'

'Well, cloves are supposed to kill the pain if you chew on them. They're those little black things you put in apple pies.'

'Have you got any?'

'There are some in the larder, on the middle shelf.'

'May I take some to my friend? They might help a bit.'

'If you like. You'll find them among the herbs and spices. They're clearly labelled.'

He looked into the larder and found them straight away, but when he opened the jar and saw how small they were his heart sank. One of those tiny black buds would be lost among Minerva's gigantic molars. 'Perhaps I'll take a few,' he said. 'They'd be better than nothing.'

'If you – I mean, your friend – really does need a dentist,' said Aunt Cis, 'we could always go to see Mr. Spruce.'

'No thanks!'

'Hmmm,' Aunt Cis looked as if she was about to say something, but thought better of it. She went to wash her hands at the sink, and said over her shoulder. 'Talking of teeth, would you like to go to the museum this afternoon, to see the dragon's tooth?'

'Oh . . . yes,' he agreed, without much enthusiasm. He supposed it would be interesting to see Minerva's tooth but he would really much rather go and see Minerva herself. Still, he would have to pretend to be interested, otherwise Aunt Cis might get suspicious.

Silverton Museum turned out to be a long, low room at the side of the vicarage. The wall was lined with books and the rest covered with glass cases containing all kinds of objects, from pieces of flint and Roman pottery to stuffed birds and animals.

52

'It's really half a library and half a museum,' explained the Vicar, who was also the curator. 'Hang on while I find the light switch.'

As soon as the cases were lit up from inside Sprog's attention was drawn to one at the far end of the room. It was by far the largest – about two metres wide and one metre high – and contained a model of the Dragon's Tooth cave, made out of papier maché. He went straight towards it.

'My showpiece,' said the Vicar, looking pleased that Sprog had noticed it so quickly. 'In there you can see the most remarkable find of all.'

Sprog stared at the interior of the cave with fascination. It was modelled in detail and for the first time he could see what it was like as a whole, instead of fragments lit up by a torch. There was the pool, made out of silver paper, in the far corner; and by the side of the pool lay the tooth, looking huge because it was out of scale to the rest of the model. And yes, it was about the same size as the other teeth he had seen in Minerva's mouth.

In front of the case was a card which read:

Interesting discovery in Laughton's Cave, now known locally as Dragon's Tooth Cave. Although this would appear to be the tooth of some prehistoric beast, the experts date it as being shed much later than that. It was discovered in 1811 by the Rev. James Coolidge, then Vicar of Silverton and the founder of this museum.

It made Sprog feel sad to look at Minerva's tooth lying there behind glass. If they did that to her tooth what would they do to Minerva herself? Surely they would not put her in a zoo! No, more likely she would be on show in the British Museum and people would come from all over the world to visit her. The queue would stretch for miles.

He felt troubled. Minerva had lived in that cave for so long without being disturbed and he did not want to be the person responsible for making her into an object of curiosity.

'Sprog, come and look at this book.' Aunt Cis was holding a slim volume with a homemade binding. 'These are all maps of the Silverton caves and the tunnels connecting them. There's one of the Dragon's Tooth Cave.'

Sprog looked down at the page she was holding towards him. 'Oh, yes,' he said politely, but his eyes were eagerly scanning the map to make sure that nothing was officially known of Minerva's tunnel. He realised at once that the shaded areas were underwater, and thought that Minerva's tunnel must go off to the left, slightly lower down than the tunnel shown on the map.

'We have one of the finest selections in the county of books about the Mendip caves,' said the Vicar with pride.

Sprog's gaze, roving rapidly over the other books, was caught by the title *The Strange World of the Dinosaurs*. His fingers itched to take it down from the shelves.

The Vicar saw he was interested and said, 'Go ahead and look at them, if you like.' Then he turned away to discuss the choice of music for Easter Sunday with Aunt Cis.

Sprog took down the book and turned over the pages, which were full of illustrations, until he came to the chapter on the duck-billed dinosaurs, and there looking at him from the page was Minerva. '*Corythosaurus*,' he read. 'About 7.5–9 metres in length, herbivorous, with a helmet-like crest. One of the last dinosaurs, becoming extinct at the end of the Cretaceous period, 65,000,000 years ago.'

It *was* Minerva, without a doubt! He suddenly realised that the Vicar and Aunt Cis had stopped talking to each other and were watching him, so went on turning the pages, pretending to look at *iguanodons*. He came to a picture of

Tyrannosaurus Rex, the Tyrant King, and shivered.

'You can stay here for a while if you like,' said Aunt Cis. 'I said I'd call in to see Mrs. Pullen, because she's offered to lend us her portable television set while you're staying with me. You'd like that, wouldn't you?'

Normally an avid television watcher, Sprog was too concerned with more urgent matters to show much interest. 'Mmmm,' he said absently. 'Actually, I promised Talker I'd help him clean the Morris this afternoon.'

'Fair enough. I'll leave you to make your own way back, then.'

He nodded, turning rather red. It wasn't that he *wanted* to tell lies or to disobey her by going up to the caves again on his own, but he really had no choice. Minerva was in pain and since he was the only human being in the world capable of understanding what was the matter with her he simply *had* to do something about it.

Chapter Seven

A Cure for Toothache

Sprog went back to Dolphin Cottage to collect the torch and the cloves. It was not so easy getting the aspirin because the bathroom cabinet was locked, but he found the key hanging on a hook in the airing cupboard. Stuffing the bottle into his pocket he locked up the cupboard again, returned the key to its hook and made his way as fast as he could to the cave.

He went in and stood by the pool, calling 'Minerva!' both with his voice and his mind.

Nothing stirred for a while but he knew she was probably in her own cave and had to swim along the sump, so he waited patiently. Just as he was about to call again the waters began to move and eventually parted as Minerva's head appeared.

'Dear boy, I'm so glad to see you!' she gasped.

'I promised I'd come. How's the toothache?'

'Quite dreadful. I've never had anything like it before. I nearly cried out with the pain but I remembered what you said so I bit on a piece of birch bark instead. I really don't know what to do next.'

He shone the torch in her direction. 'I think your face is swollen,' he said.

'Are you *sure* you can't see anything?' She turned her head to one side and opened her mouth.

He shone the torch along her jaw. This time he looked more closely because he was no longer afraid. 'I think I *can* see something. The gum looks red and sore, just there.' He touched it with his finger and Minerva drew back sharply.

'That's it,' she said, sucking in her mouth. 'What am I going to do? Oh, I'm sorry to keep on about it, but the pain is so great I can't think of anything else.'

He nodded sympathetically. 'I know what it's like. I've brought you two things, but I don't know if they'll do any good. There's some aspirin, but you'll have to take quite a few tablets, I expect. I usually take one at a time and you're about ten times larger than I am, so you'd better take ten. If you open your mouth I'll put them on your tongue.'

Obediently Minerva opened her mouth and Sprog stretched in as far as he could to put them on the back of her tongue, so they would go down more easily. He counted out ten and told her to swallow. 'It's better if you have a drink of water.'

For a few seconds she disappeared and then re-emerged, blinking the water out of her eyes. 'They're rather bitter,' she complained. 'Still, if they do any good . . . What's the other thing?'

'Cloves.' He held them out to her. 'You chew on them and they're supposed to deaden the pain. But Aunt Cis says the only real cure is to go to a dentist.'

Minerva looked blankly at him and he realised that the word dentist meant nothing to her, so he conjured up in his mind an image of the dentist's surgery and himself lying back in the chair with the hubble-bubble thing in his mouth and a white-coated figure poking away at his teeth with a sharp instrument.

'It seems to me,' said Minerva, 'that you fear this dentist as much as I fear Tyrant King.'

'I don't exactly *like* going to the dentist. Nobody does. But he makes sure you keep your teeth for as long as possible and when they fall out he makes you false ones.'

'False ones!' she exclaimed. 'I shouldn't like

that at all.'

'You won't need them,' said Sprog hastily. 'You've got very good teeth. But the dentist *does* cure toothache. You can try the cloves and the aspirins but they'll only take away the pain for a while. I'm afraid it'll come back.'

Minerva sighed deeply. Then she asked, 'How do I find a dentist?'

Sprog shook his head. 'I don't think you can. I mean, you can hardly leave your cave and go to a dentist's surgery. You'd never get inside the door.'

Minerva gave a low, despairing moan and rested her chin glumly on the floor of the cave.

'I suppose,' he said doubtfully, 'I could get one to come and see you, but how on earth would I persuade him? He'd never believe me.'

Tears began to gather in her eyes. 'Then it's quite hopeless?'

'No, it isn't. I'll get one somehow. There's even one living in the village, though I don't think . . .'

Minerva lifted her head. 'Can you make him come? *Soon*?'

Sprog took a deep breath. 'I'll do my best, but it won't be easy. I'll have to think out a plan. You see—' He hesitated. He did not want to alarm her by telling her what it would be like if people learned of her existence. Bringing a dentist to the cave was almost certain to mean a threat to her privacy.

'Bother my privacy!' said Minerva, startling him. He had forgotten she could hear his thoughts. 'Toothache is the worst thing in the world. Well, the next worst thing to Tyrant King.'

'And *he* no longer exists,' said Sprog. 'Minerva, I forgot to tell you. I know who you are. You're a *corythosaurus*.'

'Is that so?' she said, without much interest. 'Tomorrow? You'll bring the dentist tomorrow?'

'Yes, I will,' Sprog promised. 'I don't know how, but I will.'

'Dear boy!' Minerva closed her eyes briefly. 'You know, I'm beginning to feel rather sleepy.'

'It's the aspirin. You'd better go back to your cave and rest.'

'Very well.' She submerged slowly until only her eyes were showing. 'Remember – tomorrow . . .'

Sprog nodded. 'Tomorrow.'

He left the cave and walked slowly down the hillside, wondering how in the world he was going to persuade Mr. Spruce to come and look at Minerva's tooth.

Chapter Eight

The Plan

On his way down the hill Sprog noticed that he could see the roof of Mr. Spruce's house away to the left. He knew it was Mr. Spruce's house because it had a very clean, new-looking roof, whereas most of the others were brownish and moss-covered. It occurred to him that if he took a short cut through the fields behind the houses he would come out somewhere near the back garden of Dolphin Cottage.

Sure enough, after climbing over two gates and walking down a muddy track he found himself in Samson's field.

'Hello, Sprog,' said a high voice. The youngest Spruce girl was leaning over the fence, stroking Samson's nose. 'I'm talking to the horse. Isn't he lovely?'

Sprog stared at her. This, he felt, was a piece

of good luck, but he was not quite sure how to make use of it. 'Hello,' he said slowly.

'Hello, *Charley*,' she corrected. 'I called you Sprog – you have to call me Charley. You promised.'

'Hello, Charley. Where's your father?'

'He's taken Jonathan up to the Science Museum in London and Mummy's making Caroline a new dress and no one's got time to play with me.'

'Why isn't your father working?' Sprog asked. 'Is he on holiday?'

'Only for today. Tomorrow he goes back to his surgery. He's a dentist in Bristol.'

'Yes, I know.' Sprog's brain was working rapidly. If Mr. Spruce was away in Bristol all day the only time to get him to come to the cave was in the evening. That was all right: after dark would be better anyway. Perhaps he could intercept him on the way home. Aloud he asked, 'Does he travel by train?'

'Of course not!' She sounded indignant. 'He's got a car. It's a lovely car – white with a slopey front and it goes very fast.'

'What make is it, do you know?'

'I can't remember.'

'Do you know the registration number?'

'MHN —' began Charley. 'I forget the rest.'

'What time does he usually come home?'

'About seven o'clock. Mummy gets ever so cross if he's late.'

'Does he come by the main road?' He had only the vaguest idea of the route Mr. Spruce might take and was really fishing for information. Later he would find a map and work it out properly.

But Charley had grown bored with the subject. 'Oh, I don't know. The usual way. Would you like to come in and play?'

'Not now,' said Sprog. 'I've got to go and have my tea. Some other time.'

He set off across the field, thinking hard. Supposing Mr. Spruce could be persuaded to give Minerva dental treatment, would he then tell the entire world he had extracted a dinosaur's tooth? And even more important, would the entire world believe him? It might not believe Talker, with his fairy stories about dragons, but Mr. Spruce was a different matter altogether – a respected citizen and a member of the dental profession. People might take him seriously enough to make another search of the cave, to discover the tunnel they had not known existed, which meant they would almost certainly find Minerva's hiding place. How the cameras would flash, the telephones ring, the television reporters invade!

Poor Minerva.

But then, poor Minerva with toothache.

A vague plan began to form in Sprog's mind. An almost foolproof plan. But the more he thought about it the more he realised he could not manage alone. One other person would have to know about Minerva. And there was only one other person he could think of . . .

He found Talker in the barn, polishing the already gleaming bonnet of the Morris, and offered to give him a hand. As they worked he said casually, 'Talker, I need your help.'

'Oh, yes? And what can I do for you, young Sprog?'

'First, you must promise you won't tell another living soul.'

Talker looked surprised. 'Not even your Aunt Cis?'

'Not even her.'

'Well, I don't know about that . . .'

'It's *very* important.' Sprog fixed him with an earnest look. 'It's about the dragon.'

Talked stopped polishing. 'The dragon?'

'You were right – there *is* a dragon in the cave, only she's not at all fierce and she has toothache very, very badly. In fact, it was her tooth that was found years ago in the cave. Now she's got to have it out . . .'

'Hey, hold on a minute,' interrupted Talker, scratching his chin. 'You're getting me confused. How can she have a tooth out what came out years ago?'

'It's not the same tooth,' Sprog explained patiently. 'Her face is all swollen up and she's got to see a dentist, so we're going to kidnap Mr. Spruce and take him to her cave. That's why I need your help.'

Talker looked apprehensive. 'I don't know about that. Kidnapping's criminal. I'm not getting mixed up in nothing criminal. Miss Cis wouldn't like it.'

'She won't know anything about it. Anyway,

you can be disguised, if you like, so no one will recognise you. Now, this is the plan. When Mr. Spruce is driving home from Bristol I'll flag him down. Then somehow we have to persuade him to come with us up to the cave.' He had a sudden inspiration. 'Perhaps we could tell him his daughter's in danger. We could say she's got stuck in one of the caves and show him a lock of her hair as proof.'

Talker scratched his head again. 'Sounds a bit complicated to me.'

'I think it'll work, though. We shall need some brandy . . .'

'Brandy?' Talker was startled. 'What do we need brandy for?'

'Minerva must have some kind of anaesthetic, so we'll give her brandy like they did in the olden days when they were cutting off arms and legs and things and there wasn't any anaesthetic. She'll have to drink it well in advance, so we'd better take it up to her tomorrow morning.'

'And how are you going to get hold of this brandy? It's expensive stuff, you know.'

'Aunt Cis has some in a bottle in the larder. I saw it there when I was looking for the cloves. I expect it's left over from Christmas. She won't mind if we borrow a little, just enough to make Minerva unconscious.' Sprog had yet another idea. 'We could splash some of it over Mr. Spruce so that if he starts telling everyone about dino – I mean, dragons – they'll just think he's drunk. Can you get hold of some pliers?'

'Pliers?' By now Talker was completely confused.

'We'll have to give Mr. Spruce some pliers so that he can take out the tooth. Oh, and a bit of cotton wool wouldn't be a bad idea, to plug up the hole afterwards. I expect Aunt Cis has got some of that in the bathroom cabinet.' He glanced at Talker. 'You *are* going to help me, aren't you, Talker? I can't kidnap Mr. Spruce by myself.'

'Well, it's like this, young Sprog. I'm a quiet-living sort of man . . .'

'But can't you see it's important? Minerva's suffering terribly. Why don't you come with me tomorrow morning to have a look for yourself?'

'Up to that cave again?'

'Don't you want to see the dragon? You're always telling other people stories about it.'

'It's not just the dragon,' Talker admitted reluctantly. 'It's that ghost as well.'

Sprog thought quickly. 'But the ghost is only there to protect the secret of the cave. If you help the dragon the ghost will be on your side. In fact, I wouldn't be surprised if he didn't make sure you had a piece of real good luck.'

Talker brightened. 'You mean, like a win on the football pools?'

'Something like that,' said Sprog vaguely. 'It'll be on condition you keep it a secret, of course. The ghost won't like it if you go around telling everyone.'

'I shan't tell a soul,' Talker assured him.

Sprog found that rather difficult to believe, but he could only hope that the sight of poor Minerva's swollen face would persuade the old man to help them.

Chapter Nine

Talker Meets the Dragon

Next morning Sprog climbed up to the hayloft, waving a half-full bottle of brandy. 'I've got it!' he shouted triumphantly. 'And I've poured some into a smaller bottle to throw over Mr. Spruce, so Minerva can drink all of this.'

Talker, who was in the middle of pulling on his boots, stopped to stare at him.

'I've already told Aunt Cis we're going to the caves,' Sprog went on. 'She says it's okay.'

'Maybe she does,' grumbled Talker, doing up his laces, 'but she don't know we're taking a bottle of her brandy with us, does she?'

'Come on! We'll take the short cut I discovered yesterday.' Sprog took hold of his arm and dragged him, protesting, out of the barn, through the garden and across Samson's field.

When they reached the Dragon's Tooth Cave Talker hung back obstinately. 'I'm not going in there,' he said. 'This is far enough.'

'You must come in if you want to see the dragon. She won't hurt you, I promise.'

Unwillingly Talker allowed himself to be led into the cave, but he refused to go anywhere near the pool. 'Well? Where is it, then?' he demanded.

'I'll have to call her.' Sprog directed his thoughts along the tunnel while holding on firmly to the fringe of Talker's coat in case the old man bolted at his first sight of Minerva.

After a few moments the waters of the pool began to heave. Talker gave a moan and started to back away, but Sprog held him fast. When Minerva's head appeared Talker covered his eyes with his hands.

'You must look!' urged Sprog.

Minerva, startled by the apparition of Talker moaning and backing away from her, prepared to submerge again.

'Minerva, please don't go!' called Sprog. 'It's only Talker. He's scared stiff, but we need his help if I'm to get you a dentist.'

Minerva hesitated. 'Why is he covering his eyes like that?' she asked curiously.

'He's afraid to look at you.'

'Well, that's not very polite, I must say!'

Sprog, still struggling with Talker, managed to shine the torch in her direction. 'I think your face is more swollen than ever!' he exclaimed.

'It's absolute agony, dear boy. I've had a terrible time. I slept for a while – it must have been those pills you gave me – but as soon as I woke up it started again. When's the dentist coming?'

'Tonight, about seven o'clock.'

'Let me go!' shouted Talker, whose voice at least had recovered from the shock, though he still kept his eyes covered.

'If only you'd look at her!' said Sprog, exasperated.

'I *have* looked!' spluttered Talker. 'I've seen it . . . with my own eyes I've seen the dragon! Now let me go.'

'All right.' Cautiously Sprog released his coat. 'But don't go too far away.'

Talker backed until he touched the cave wall behind him, then felt his way along it towards the entrance. 'I'll wait outside,' he said in a wavering voice.

'I shan't be long,' Sprog promised.

He returned to the pool to find only Minerva's eyes above water level. She raised her head as he came nearer. 'What an odd fellow! Is he really going to help us?'

'I hope so.' He fished in his pocket for the bottle of brandy. 'I've brought this for you to take. It'll deaden the pain so you won't feel Mr. Spruce take the tooth out.'

Minerva reached out a skinny arm to take hold of the bottle and opened her huge mouth ready to drop it in.

'No, you don't swallow the whole bottle!' Sprog managed to grab it from her in time. 'You're supposed to take the top off first.'

He showed her how to unscrew the lid. 'Don't drink it too early,' he warned. 'Just before seven o'clock will be about the right time.'

'How shall I know when it's seven o'clock?'

'You'd better keep looking out of the cave and drink it when it begins to get dark.'

'All right.' She unscrewed the lid and sniffed at the contents. 'Pooh! I don't care much for the smell.'

'People drink that for pleasure,' he told her. 'They put it in puddings and things.'

'There's no accounting for taste.' She replaced the lid and sighed. 'I'm beginning to feel rather nervous. There are flutterings in my stomach.'

'Butterflies. Everyone has butterflies when they're going to see the dentist.' Sprog glanced at the cave entrance. 'I'd better go now because of Talker. Remember, as soon as it begins to get dark drink all the brandy and wait here in the cave for us.'

'I really don't know how to thank you, dear boy.' There was a suspicion of moisture in her eye.

'Well, I've a few more details to work out yet,' he said cautiously. 'But don't worry, we'll get Mr. Spruce here somehow.'

'Too kind,' she murmured as she sank beneath the dark waters of the pool.

Outside the cave Talker was resting on a boulder. When Sprog emerged from the entrance he clambered shakily to his feet and inquired, 'You wouldn't by any chance have that spare drop of brandy on you, I suppose? I don't feel so good.'

''Fraid not,' said Sprog. 'Anyway, we're going to need that to sprinkle over Mr. Spruce. There's just one thing that bothers me and that's stopping the right car.'

Talker gave a sniff. 'It's one of them modern jobs – all flash and no class.'

'Would you recognise it if you saw it coming along the road?'

'Oh, yes, I'd know it all right. Nearly ran into the Morris once, he did. Drives round these lanes like they were the motorway.'

'In that case you can warn me when he's coming. What we need is a lookout post not too far away, so that after you've given me the signal you can come back to help with the kidnapping.'

Talker thought for a moment. 'I reckon there's a spot a bit further down this hill that would do.'

'Show me,' said Sprog.

Still a little unsteady on his feet, Talker led the way down the hill, veering off to the right. Sure enough, there was a vantage point about thirty feet above the road which gave a commanding view of the surrounding countryside and the road to Silverton.

'Just what we wanted,' said Sprog, pleased. 'Now I'll go down to the road, just round the corner, and you wave when you can see me.'

He scrambled down the hillside. When he reached the road he turned and looked up the hill. There was no sign of Talker. Sprog gave a yell and Talker's face appeared suddenly over a clump of bushes. He waved an arm and then disappeared again.

Sprog climbed back up the hill to find the old man lying back on the grass, taking a rest.

'Me legs gave way,' Talker explained. 'I'm not used to all this running up and down hills and meeting dragons and suchlike. Me old heart's banging away like a drum.'

Sprog looked at him anxiously. The old man really had turned a little grey. 'The lookout's

okay, anyway,' he said. 'I can certainly see you from there and in the dark it'll be easier because you'll be able to signal to me with the torch. It's a good thing the car's white because it'll show up well.' He stretched out a hand. 'Come on. I'll give you some help.'

With Talker leaning heavily upon his shoulder, Sprog made his way back to Dolphin Cottage. As they entered the kitchen Aunt Cis looked up and her expression grew concerned when she saw Talker's face. 'Come and sit down,' she said quickly. 'I've got some brandy in the larder . . .'

Hastily Sprog gave Talker a nudge and Talker raised his head to say, 'Er, no – no thanks. I don't feel like brandy. A cup of tea would do me nicely.'

Aunt Cis looked surprised. 'If you say so.' She put the kettle on the hob and said to Sprog in a low voice, 'What caused it?'

'I think the walk up the hill was too much for him.'

'He's always been fit as a fiddle. It looks more like a case of shock to me.' In a louder voice she added, 'By the way, did you see there was a letter for you on the hall table?'

Sprog opened the airmail envelope and found two letters inside, one from his mother and the other from his brother, Francis. His mother said things were a little better: the airport had re-opened but they still had to be careful about going out. She went on to say how upset she was that Sprog couldn't be with them, but she was sure it was all for the best and hoped he was managing to have a good time with Aunt Cis.

The note from Francis was short and untidy. 'Things are a bit dangrus here,' he wrote. 'We havnt been swiming and it is verey hot. I hope it is not boring in Ingland. It is not boring here. But I wish we cood swim. From Francis.'

Reading this, Sprog grinned. 'Oh, no,' he muttered to himself. 'Things are not boring here. Not boring at all!'

Chapter Ten

Hide and Seek

'What are your plans for this afternoon?' inquired Aunt Cis when they were having lunch.

'I thought I might go over to the Spruces' house,' said Sprog.

Aunt Cis looked surprised. 'Really? Well, I hope they turn out to be more friendly than last time.'

'Oh, they're not *all* unfriendly,' said Sprog, quite truthfully.

After lunch he walked through Samson's field until he came to the fence at the bottom of the Spruces' garden. He had no real plan of action, but intended to grasp whatever opportunity came his way.

It seemed at first that luck was not on his side. There were no signs of life at all in the house or the garden.

Sprog waited for a few minutes and then gave a low whistle, crouching down behind the fence. Cautiously he raised his head and looked at the house. Nothing stirred. He whistled again, louder this time, and saw a window open on the top floor. Charley's head appeared.

He stood up and waved. Charley waved back and beckoned him to come over.

'Oh good, you've come to play,' she called as soon as he was within earshot. 'Jonathan and Caroline have gone out riding and I'm up here by myself. Mummy's lying down 'cos her eyes

are tired.' She leaned out as far as she could over the window-sill. 'Shall I be that princess who lets down her hair for you to climb up?'

Sprog groaned inwardly. 'I wouldn't get very far,' he growled, looking up at her short curls.

'All right . . . wait a minute.' She disappeared briefly and seconds later reappeared wearing a long blonde wig, with a fringe that almost covered her eyes.

'That's not much better,' said Sprog. Then it occurred to him that a wig would be useful for Talker's disguise. 'Have you any others?' he asked.

'Heaps!' Charley snatched off the blonde wig and replaced it with a straggly grey one. 'Oh dear, that won't reach either. You'll have to come up the stairs.'

'What about your mother?'

'She's asleep. I'll come down and let you in.'

He waited until she appeared from a side door. 'Come on!' she hissed, grabbing him by the arm. 'We can play at acting. I've got a whole big dressing-up box upstairs.'

He allowed himself to be pulled through a clean and orderly kitchen smelling faintly of disinfectant. The hall and stairs were carpeted so their feet made no sound at all, but when they reached the landing Charley put her finger to her lips. 'We'd better creep past Mummy's room,' she whispered.

'Is that you, dear?' called a weary voice. 'What are you doing?'

Through the open doorway Sprog could see into a darkened room where Mrs. Spruce lay on the bed, with white pads over her eyes.

'It's just a friend come to play,' Charley replied.

'Who is it, dear?'

'Susan Barnes,' said Charley without so much as a flicker of an eyelid. When Sprog looked at her in surprise she put a finger to her lips.

'How lovely,' sighed Mrs. Spruce. 'Run along, then, and leave Mummy in peace.'

'Come on, Susan,' said Charley loudly, pushing Sprog into the playroom. When the door was closed behind them she said, 'I didn't tell her who you were because of that fight you had with Jonathan. There was blood on his sleeve afterwards.'

'Mine,' said Sprog.

'Anyway, she didn't like it. She said you were a nasty rough boy and we weren't to have anything more to do with you.'

Stung though he was by the injustice of this remark, Sprog began to feel elated. Good luck was certainly on his side, he thought as he stared down at the dressing-up box full of wigs and masks and other such useful disguises. 'Have you any beards or anything like that?' he asked, thinking that a beard would disguise Talker's face beyond all recognition.

'I think so. Let's have a look.'

They rummaged through the chest and while Charley decked herself out with feathers and festoons of paper flowers Sprog managed to find a grey beard that would be exactly right.

'Who am I?' called Charley, dancing around in front of him. 'You've got to guess who I am.'

'King Kong,' said Sprog absently, wondering how he was going to get hold of a lock of her hair.

'No, silly! Hansel and Gretel. Now it's your turn.'

Half-heartedly he pulled a black balaclava over his head and swung round to face Charley, holding an imaginary gun at arm's length. 'Okay, stick 'em up and tell me who I am.'

'That's easy,' she said. 'Robin Hood.'

He groaned and pulled off the balaclava in disgust. 'This is hopeless. We don't watch the same TV programmes.'

'There's lots of other games in here.' She opened the door of a cupboard to reveal shelves of neatly stacked cardboard boxes. 'You can choose one, if you like.'

He pretended to inspect the games closely while trying to think what he could take to prove to Mr. Spruce that his daughter was in danger. If he snipped off one of Charley's curls she'd be bound to tell her mother. No, he needed something that belonged to her . . . something she could have lost in the cave . . .

'How about a game of hide-and-seek?' he suggested.

Charley looked uncertain. 'Mummy mightn't like it. She'd say we were being noisy.'

'Not if we play it silently. You can stay in here and count to a hundred while I go off and hide.'

'Oh, all right,' she agreed reluctantly.

'You mustn't look. That would be cheating.'

Obediently she closed her eyes and began counting. Sprog seized the beard and the grey wig and stuffed them inside his sweater. He crept furtively out of the playroom and along the landing.

He tried a door and found himself inside a pink-and-white bedroom, which he guessed must belong to Caroline. His eye fell on a pair of slippers under the bed. One of Caroline's shoes would do very well, he thought: after all, it didn't matter which daughter was in danger. But slippers were no good. She would hardly be exploring a cave in slippers.

He opened a fitted cupboard and found a rack of clean, feminine shoes. He selected one of them and carefully closed the door again.

As he went back on to the landing Mrs. Spruce called out, 'Is that you, girls? Are you having a game?'

Sprog made his voice high and squeaky. 'It's me . . . Susan,' he piped. 'We're playing hide-and-seek.'

'That's nice,' murmured Mrs. Spruce. 'Don't make the house in a mess, will you?'

'We won't,' squeaked Sprog.

Clutching Caroline's shoe under his arm he went downstairs. Charley must be dangerously near the hundred mark by now. He went through the side door and ran across the garden, bent double to make himself less conspicuous.

As soon as he was safely over the fence he let out a whoop of triumph and ran back to Dolphin Cottage.

He went straight up to his room and hid the shoe and Talker's disguise at the bottom of the wardrobe.

Aunt Cis looked up when he joined her in the sitting room. 'You didn't stay long.'

'There was no one there except the youngest girl,' said Sprog. 'Oh, and a friend of hers called Susan Barnes.'

Chapter Eleven

The Kidnapping of Mr. Spruce

After tea Sprog went upstairs and checked over the items needed for the kidnapping of Mr. Spruce: Caroline's shoe, the wig and the beard, the remains of the brandy in an old aspirin bottle, the cotton wool . . .

What he wanted was something large to wave at Mr. Spruce. If the white car should pass too quickly without noticing him the whole plan would fail. He took the pillow-slip off his bed and put the other articles inside it.

He found Talker in the hayloft, cooking baked beans on a primus stove. 'Look, I've brought you a disguise,' he said, showing him the wig and the beard. 'Try them on and see what you look like.'

Talker tried them on. The beard was on a piece of elastic and kept slipping up under his nose, but the wig fitted him perfectly and made him look like a weird old wizard.

'You can't possibly wear your own coat,' said Sprog. 'Everyone would recognise that. Haven't you got something else?'

Talker scratched his head. 'There's an old nurse's cloak Miss Cis gave me to put over me bed of a winter's night. Navy blue it is, with a red lining. I think it's around here somewhere . . .'

Sprog pulled off a couple of blankets and found the cloak underneath, looking somewhat creased and dusty. 'That'll be just right. Put it on.'

Talker wrapped himself in the cloak and Sprog looked him over critically. The disguise certainly altered his appearance.

'We must remember to take the torch for signalling.' He frowned anxiously. 'I wish we had a better light for the operation, though, so that Mr. Spruce can see what he's doing.'

'There's an old paraffin lamp down in the barn,' said Talker. 'It gives out a good strong light.'

'Right! We'll take it. How about paraffin?'

'Plenty of that in the can.'

'We'll fill it now, so that it's ready. Aunt Cis takes choir practice tonight so she'll be out of the way. I reckon we ought to be up there on the hill by six forty-five. All we need now are the pliers.'

They had to go down the steps to the barn to find the pliers and while they were there they filled the paraffin lamp. 'I'll bring some matches,' said Sprog. 'You've only got three things to remember – beard, wig and cloak. Okay?'

He left Talker still muttering to himself and returned to the cottage, where he went upstairs and shut himself in the bathroom. He knew that surgical instruments ought to be sterilised in boiling water but did not see how he could put the kettle on without Aunt Cis noticing, so he cleaned the pliers as best he could under the hot tap.

He felt quite pleased with himself when he finally sat down with Aunt Cis in front of the television to watch the early evening news. Really the whole plan was a masterpiece of organisation!

But as time went on he began to feel nervous. There was so much that could go wrong.

Aunt Cis glanced at her watch. 'I'd better be on my way up to the church hall,' she said, getting to her feet. 'I'll just collect the torch . . .

For a moment Sprog was paralysed. Then he sprang to his feet. 'I'll get it for you.'

He rushed into the hall and took the torch

down from the shelf.

When it was safely hidden in the pocket of his anorak he went back to the sitting room. 'I can't find it anywhere.'

'You didn't by any chance leave it up in the caves?'

'I may have done,' he said vaguely. 'I'm terribly sorry.'

'Don't worry. I can manage without it. Sure you wouldn't like to come with me?'

'Quite sure, thanks.'

When the door had closed behind her he drew in a deep breath. Now that the moment had come for action he felt both excited and icy calm at the same time. He collected the pillow-slip from his room and went over to the barn.

He met Talker coming furtively down the steps from the hayloft. The old man jumped when he saw him. 'Just thought I'd slip down to the George and Dragon for a quick pint,' he said.

'There isn't time. Where's your disguise?'

Grumbling, Talker climbed back up to the hayloft and reappeared wearing the nurse's cloak but carrying the wig and the beard. 'I'll put these on later,' he said. 'They're too scratchy to wear all the time.'

Sprog gave him the torch. 'You'll need that for signalling. I'll carry the lamp.'

They took the short cut through the field and soon reached the lookout point.

'It's lighter than I expected,' Sprog said anxiously, remembering he had told Minerva not to take the brandy until it was getting dark. 'Still, at least it'll make the car easier to see. I'd better go down to the road now. Give me the signal as soon as you see him.'

Sprog reached the road and positioned himself behind a bush, from where he had a good view of Talker. He put the paraffin lamp on the ground for the time being and emptied the things out of the pillow-slip, concealing the brandy, matches, pliers and cotton wool about his person. Now he was ready to leap into the road, holding the shoe in one hand and the pillow-slip in the other.

When it got to 7.10 p.m. he had a sinking feeling in his stomach. Supposing Mr. Spruce had taken a different route or maybe even come home early for a change? Just then he saw the torch flashing. He gripped the pillow-slip firmly and stepped out into the road. Headlights came towards him. Frantically he waved the pillow-slip but the car showed no sign of slowing down.

'Stop!' yelled Sprog. 'Help! It's a matter of life and death.'

Although his shouts could not possibly be heard by the driver, the desperation on his face must have been convincing because at last the car squealed to a halt.

Mr. Spruce wound down his window. 'What's going on?' he asked, as Sprog arrived beside him.

'It's your daughter,' panted Sprog. 'Caroline. We were playing in the caves and she slipped. Jonathan's stayed with her but I came down to try and stop you. We knew you'd be coming along at about this time—'

'Is that her shoe?' interrupted Mr. Spruce.

'Oh . . . yes.' He had almost forgotten his proof. 'She dropped it.'

'You young idiots!' Mr. Spruce's expression was thunderous. 'Which cave is it? I'll take the car home and come straight up.'

'There isn't time for that,' said Sprog quickly. 'You ought to come now. It's only just over there . . . at the top of the hill.'

Mr. Spruce glanced up. 'All right. I'll pull into the side of the road.'

He moved the car a few metres farther on and managed to park it off the road, on some gravel. He got out and slammed the door. 'Right,' he said grimly. 'Now show me where those stupid children of mine have got themselves into this mess!'

Sprog picked up the lamp and led the way up the hillside, hoping that Talker was not too far

behind them.

As soon as they reached the cave entrance Mr. Spruce demanded, 'Well? Where is she?'

'We need some light,' said Sprog, looking over his shoulder. To his relief Talker's shadow appeared, the torch held in his wavering hand.

'Jonathan, is that you?' inquired Mr. Spruce, turning round.

When he received no reply he seized the torch and directed the beam at Talker, illuminating a strange figure, wig slightly askew and beard under his nose. 'What the devil . . . ?'

'Stay outside and keep watch,' Sprog hissed urgently to Talker. 'Whistle if anyone comes.'

'Is this a joke?' asked Mr. Spruce. 'Where's Caroline?'

'If you wait a moment you'll be able to see.' Sprog struggled to light the paraffin lamp.

But Mr. Spruce was already striding into the cave, using the torch to light his way. As soon as the lamp was safely lit Sprog followed him.

The lamp's strong glow filled the cave, revealing the huge shape of Minerva, who had climbed out of the pool and was waiting for them, leaning against the wall of the cave.

'Good evening,' she said politely.

Mr. Spruce stared at her for one horrified moment and then fell down in a dead faint.

Chapter Twelve

Operation Toothache

'Why is he lying down?' asked Minerva. 'Is he tired?'

'I expect it's the shock,' said Sprog. 'He's probably never seen a dinosaur before and you are rather large, you know.' He knelt beside Mr. Spruce, loosening his collar.

Minerva hiccuped and gazed disdainfully down at the supine figure at her feet. 'Silly old dentist!'

Sprog looked up at her suspiciously. 'I think you're a bit drunk. I suppose it was the brandy.'

'I do feel rather odd,' she admitted.

'Brandy!' exclaimed Sprog, remembering the small bottle in his pocket. Quickly he poured some into Mr. Spruce's open mouth. It dribbled out again over his collar and Sprog sprinkled the rest over his jacket. 'That should do the trick.'

Mr. Spruce spluttered and opened his eyes, blinking rapidly. Sprog helped him into a sitting position. 'Put your head between your knees,' he ordered. 'You'll feel better in a minute.'

'What happened?' murmured Mr. Spruce.

'You fainted because you saw a dragon,' Sprog explained. 'I'm sorry I had to trick you into coming here by pretending your daughter was in danger, but you'd never have listened to me otherwise.'

At this point Mr. Spruce took his second look at Minerva. 'Great heavens! Am I seeing things?'

'No, there really is a dragon, but the trouble is she has toothache. That's why I brought you here, so that you can take the tooth out.'

Mr. Spruce went on gazing at Minerva. 'Amazing . . .!'

'She's in a great deal of pain,' said Sprog. 'I know you've probably never treated a dragon before . . .'

'Young man, that is no dragon!' said Mr. Spruce, getting to his feet. 'A hadrosaur . . . one of the crested variety. I must look it up. Fascinating . . . absolutely fascinating! Living in these caves . . . It must be something like 60 million years . . .'

'Can't you see that her face is swollen?' asked Sprog desperately. 'Minerva, open your mouth and show him your teeth.'

Obediently Minerva opened her mouth wide and Mr. Spruce took a step backwards. Then his curiosity got the better of him and he moved closer.

'It's on the left-hand side,' said Sprog, holding the lamp near.

'I can see!' snapped Mr. Spruce. 'I suspect an abscess under the tooth. It should come out.'

Sprog sighed with relief. 'As soon as possible, please. You don't have to worry about tools. I've brought some for you.'

'Tools!' exclaimed Mr. Spruce, affronted. '*Tools*! I shall need special surgical instruments for this operation. It will make medical history! We must give scientific observers an opportunity to be present. They'll come from all over the world.' He added excitedly, half to himself, 'This will be the crowning achievement of my career!'

'Minerva, you'd better move forward,' said Sprog. 'We'll have to cut off his exit from the cave.'

'Why doesn't he get on with it?' she grumbled. 'I'm beginning to feel nervous again.' She lumbered forward, effectively sealing off the only way of escape, and Mr. Spruce turned a little pale.

Sprog pulled the pliers from his pocket. 'Here

you are,' he said, holding them out. 'I have washed them.'

'Pliers?' Mr. Spruce stared at them, shocked.

'And I've got some cotton wool if you need it. She's already had some brandy to deaden the pain.'

'I thought I could smell it.' Mr. Spruce sniffed the air, apparently not realising that most of the smell was coming from his own coat. He held the pliers at arm's length with a disgusted look on his face. 'I can't use these!' he declared. 'I must have the right instruments.'

'For goodness' sake!' said Sprog impatiently. 'Pulling a tooth out isn't *that* complicated! You just give it a tug and out it comes.'

'I don't need you to tell me my job, young man.' Mr. Spruce frowned. 'But it'll hurt. A wounded animal that size . . .' he eyed Minerva uneasily, 'could turn vicious. It's already trapped us in here, do you realise that?'

'Only because I told her to,' said Sprog.

'Oh, so you can talk to it, can you?' said Mr. Spruce scornfully.

Minerva yawned. 'I shall go to sleep in a minute,' she said. 'Tell him to hurry up.'

The sight of Minerva yawning sent Mr. Spruce stumbling back against the side of the cave.

'She's getting bored,' said Sprog. 'You'd

97

better get it over quickly.' He turned to Minerva. 'Open wide.'

Minerva stretched her long neck towards Mr. Spruce and opened her jaw so that the offending tooth was in a convenient position. Mr. Spruce stared at it helplessly, weighing the pliers in his hand. 'Did you say you had some cotton wool?' he asked.

Sprog retrieved it from under his sweater and held it out.

'Make a roll about the size of a cigar. We'll need it to plug the hole. I hope it's clean.'

'Of course it's clean!' said Sprog indignantly. 'It's all done up in blue paper.'

Very slowly Mr. Spruce moved the pliers towards Minerva's tooth. 'If you really can talk to this thing you'd better warn it this is going to hurt.'

'You must be brave,' Sprog told Minerva. 'He says it will hurt. I'll hold your hand, if you like.'

'Dear boy,' sighed Minerva, reaching out a claw. 'You're such a comfort!'

Mr. Spruce drew in a deep breath and fastened the pliers around the tooth. He gave a professional twist of the wrist and the tooth moved slightly. Minerva's tail twitched.

The sweat began to pour down Mr. Spruce's face. He took a firmer hold and pulled again.

There was an unpleasant wrenching sound and the tooth came away cleanly.

'Cotton wool,' commanded Mr. Spruce.

'Cotton wool,' repeated Sprog, holding out the ready-made plug.

'I think I'm going to faint,' said Minerva weakly.

'No, you mustn't do that. Hold on . . . it won't take a moment now.'

'But I'm bleeding!' she moaned.

'Not very much,' said Sprog in a bracing tone. 'There! Now you're all plugged up. That wasn't so bad, was it?'

'It was the worst experience of my life!' Minerva moved her jaw about experimentally.

Sprog looked round just in time to see Mr. Spruce taking the tooth from the grip of the pliers. 'Sorry,' he said, holding out his hand, 'but you'll have to give that to me.'

'I shall do nothing of the sort!' said Mr. Spruce, examining it carefully. 'This tooth is going to be my prime exhibit. I shall have it mounted and hang it on the wall of my surgery.'

Sprog's heart sank. 'Surely you can understand that we must keep this a secret?' he pleaded. 'Poor Minerva's life would be a misery if people found out about her. Reporters, scientists, sightseers – she'd never have a moment's peace.'

A gleam came into Mr. Spruce's eye. 'You're surely not suggesting we should keep this discovery to ourselves? This creature,' he waved a hand at Minerva, 'belongs to the nation. It belongs to mankind!'

'She belongs to herself!' said Sprog, turning pink with anger. 'She has a right to privacy, same as anyone else.'

'Young man, you are mad!' Mr. Spruce's expression grew cunning. 'What did you say your name was, by the way?'

'Er, Francis.' He said the first name that came into his head, which happened to be his brother's. Then he added, for good measure, 'Drake.'

'Francis Drake . . . a famous name indeed!' said Mr. Spruce in ringing tones. 'A name that will echo round the world, together with my own, of course. We shall go down in the history books, my young friend.'

'I think I'd better remind you,' said Sprog quietly, 'that you can't get out of this cave until I tell Minerva to move. What's more, if I give the word she could break every bone in your body. One lash of her tail would be enough.'

'It's no good threatening me.' Mr. Spruce threw out his chest aggressively. 'I'm not afraid.'

'Why does he keep shouting?' complained Minerva. 'I'm getting the most awful headache. Can't we let him go now?'

'Not until he's given us back your tooth – and the pliers. Minerva, do you think you could knock them out of his hand with your tail?'

'I'll try, dear boy.' Minerva gave a flick of her tail that sent Mr. Spruce flying across the cave floor. 'Goodness,' she said apologetically. 'I'm afraid I was a bit rough. I didn't mean to knock him over.'

'That's all right.' Sprog seized the pliers and the tooth from the floor, where they had fallen. 'You just don't know your own strength, that's all.' He turned to Mr. Spruce, who was looking dazed and rubbing his arm. 'Are you all right, sir?'

'I think so.' Mr. Spruce felt himself all over. 'What hit me?'

'Minerva's tail. I did warn you.'

Mr. Spruce struggled to his feet. 'I want to get out of here before that thing murders me,' he said fearfully.

'Let him go,' Sprog told Minerva, and she shuffled backwards to leave the entrance clear.

In one bound Mr. Spruce shot through the gap and disappeared.

Chapter Thirteen

Covering Tracks

'Now he'll tell everyone!' Sprog looked anxiously at Minerva. 'You can't possibly stay here.'

She blinked. 'But where can I go?'

'I'll have to take you down to Dolphin Cottage. You should just about fit into the barn, with a bit of luck.'

Minerva looked as if she were about to cry. 'But I don't want to leave my cave.'

'It's only for a while, until the fuss has died down,' he said hastily, 'then you'll be able to come back.'

She sighed. 'Oh, well . . . if you say so, Sprog.'

He went to the cave entrance and called out to Talker, who appeared cautiously from behind a boulder, still wearing his disguise.

'We've got to take Minerva home with us,'

Sprog told him. 'She'll have to hide in the barn, so you'd better go on ahead and move the Morris out of the way.'

Talker glanced into the cave and turned pale. 'The dragon? In our barn? Miss Cis won't like that!'

'She won't mind if it's an emergency. Go on. Hurry!'

Grumbling to himself, Talker set off down the hill. Sprog turned back to the cave. 'Minerva!' he called. 'Are you coming?'

She squeezed through the entrance and stood outside, swaying slightly. 'I'm feeling *most* peculiar . . .'

'We must get away from the cave before Mr. Spruce has time to give the alarm. Come on, and try not to tread too heavily. We don't want to leave tracks.'

She ambled down the path at what seemed to Sprog a painfully slow pace. It was now so dark he was unable to see whether or not she was leaving a trail behind her, but fortunately the ground was fairly hard.

When they reached the field behind the Spruces' house he noticed there were lights in every window. Mr. Spruce must be making quite a fuss, he thought.

The sight and scent of Minerva sent Samson

whinnying and galloping round his field. Sprog went over to lay a soothing hand on his mane. 'It's all right,' he said in thought language. 'She won't do you any harm.'

At last the old horse was calm enough to be led over to the far side of the field, where he stood quivering and snorting. Sprog returned to Minerva.

'What do you call that creature?' she asked. 'There weren't any of them about in my day.'

'It's a horse.'

'Fine looking little beast, but rather highly-strung, I thought.'

'That's only natural. He's never seen a dinosaur before.'

'Well, I've never seen a horse before, but I'm not making a song-and-dance about it!' she remarked with a sniff.

The real problem came when they reached the wicker gate that led into Aunt Cis's vegetable garden. Sprog could see no way in without breaking down the gate posts. 'Could you try stepping over the fence?' he suggested.

'I'll do my best, dear boy,' said Minerva. She stepped carefully over and then toppled forward on to her short arms in order to lift her tail as far as possible off the ground. Sprog tried not to look as she made her way through the vegetable garden. Fortunately it was too early in the year for her to do too much damage, but as they rounded the corner she accidentally flattened a rhododendron bush.

When they reached the barn Sprog whispered, 'Wait here,' and pushed open the side door.

'Talker,' he called in a low voice. 'Where are you?'

Talker appeared, minus disguise but with his hand over his eyes. 'Is the dragon there?' he asked nervously.

'Yes, she's here. Have you moved the car?'

'I've left it round the corner in the layby so that Miss Cis won't see it on her way back from choir practice. Otherwise she'd wonder what it was doing out in the drive.'

'Good thinking! Have you left the doors open? I'll bring Minerva round to the front.'

'Here, let me get out of the way first! I'm not hanging around in here with no dragons.' With his eyes still covered Talker slid through the door and edged away into the darkness.

'That man's getting on my nerves,' said Minerva. 'You'd think I was ugly, the way he avoids looking at me!'

'The less he looks at you the safer you are,' Sprog pointed out. 'As long as he thinks you're a dragon no one's going to believe him. The real danger is Mr. Spruce. He guessed exactly what you were. In fact, the sooner we get you hidden the better.'

He led her round the side of the barn and in through the double doors. She had to stoop to get inside, but once there she fitted in quite snugly.

'I like it,' she said, looking about her. 'Yes, I like it very much.' She stretched her neck through the hole where the steps went up to the loft. 'There's even an extra room up here for my head.'

'Be careful you don't get stuck,' warned Sprog. 'Will you be all right if I leave you now? I still have a few things to see to.'

'Carry on, dear boy. I shall be perfectly comfortable here.'

He returned the paraffin lamp to its corner and the pliers to the shelf. Then he felt inside his pocket to make sure the tooth was safe. Relieved that all seemed to be well he closed the doors and went into the kitchen, where he found Talker making himself a cup of tea.

'And where am *I* going to sleep tonight?' demanded the old man as soon as he saw Sprog. 'That's what I'd like to know!'

'Minerva won't mind in the least if you squeeze past her up to the hayloft.'

Talker looked horrified. 'What? Me stay in there with a dragon popping up its head every few seconds to breathe fire over me? I'd never sleep a wink!' He sighed. 'I suppose it'll have to be the back seat of the Morris. At least she's a comfortable old car, not like one of them modern jobs.'

'What have you done with your disguise?' asked Sprog. 'We've got to get rid of all the evidence.'

Talker fumbled in his pocket and produced the wig and the beard. Sprog took them from him and stared at them. 'Talker, I've just had the most brilliant idea! When Mr. Spruce left the cave he ran straight home, didn't he?'

Talker nodded. 'Certainly did! Went down that hill like a hundred devils were after him!'

'That means his car is still down by the road, where he left it. Supposing I shove these things on the back seat? It will make it look like a practical joke! No one will believe him then . . .'

Talker looked doubtful. 'While you're about it, you ought to return that girl's shoe as well. Otherwise it'll be stealing.'

Sprog turned pale. 'Caroline's shoe . . .' he said slowly. 'It's still in the cave . . . and so's the pillow-slip! Talker, I'll have to go back!'

On his way through the field it occurred to him that if he took Samson along the old horse's large hoof marks would help cover up any tracks Minerva might have left. He took hold of Samson's halter and explained to him what was happening. Then he led him up the hillside, taking care to retrace the route exactly.

When they reached the cave he told Samson to wait outside. The pillow-slip and Caroline's shoe were lying exactly where he had left them. He folded the pillow-slip as small as possible and put it inside his sweater. He tried hiding the shoe there as well but it was too uncomfortable, so he held it in his hand while he scuffed about in the dust to remove any sign of footprints or claw-marks.

No sooner had he come out of the cave and taken hold of Samson's halter than he heard sounds of movement and saw a dark shape looming up in front of him.

'And what might you be up to, young man?' asked a deep voice. In the moonlight Sprog could just make out the unmistakeable outline of a policeman's helmet. Quickly he concealed the shoe behind his back.

The policeman shone his torch over the boy and the horse.

'Surely that's old Samson, Mr. Priddy's

horse!' he exclaimed.

'That's right,' said Sprog. 'He got out of his field. I just chased him up the hill.'

The policeman came nearer and patted the horse's neck. 'Fancy that! Wouldn't have thought there was that much life left in the old fellow.' He studied Sprog closely. 'Don't think we've met before, have we? Are you new to the village?'

'Just staying here for the holidays with my great aunt – Miss Cissie Stokes.'

'Ah, I remember!' The policeman nodded. 'Well, my lad, you'd best get on home. Not a very safe place at this time of night, these caves. Oh, there's just one question I'd like to ask you before you go.'

Sprog waited, holding his breath.

'Don't suppose you've seen anything odd, have you, while you've been up here?'

'What sort of thing?' inquired Sprog.

'It's just that we've had a report . . .' The policeman broke off and gave a short laugh. 'I daresay it's one of these jokers up to their tricks. I'll have to take a look around, though, just in case.' He shone his torch over the cave entrance. 'Off you go, then. Mind you take that horse straight back to his field.'

'Yes, sir.'

Sprog led Samson down the hill, grinning to himself. He could just imagine what kind of a report the police had received!

As soon as he had returned Samson to his field he took the short cut over the hillside to the road. The car was there all right, by the side of the road, and as he hoped Mr. Spruce had left the door unlocked in his haste to reach his daughter. Sprog threw the beard, wig and shoe onto the back seat and carefully wiped his fingerprints from the door handle.

When he returned to Dolphin Cottage he looked into the barn and saw a huge mound in the darkness. There came the sound of heavy, rhythmic breathing. He closed the door again quietly in order not to waken Minerva and went back into the cottage.

The next morning Aunt Cis came up to his room early and drew back the curtains. He rubbed his eyes and peered at her.

'Perhaps you wouldn't mind explaining to me,' she said calmly, 'why there's a dinosaur asleep in my barn?'

Chapter Fourteen

A Fly on the Wall

'Is there anything in the newspaper?' asked Sprog.

They were still sitting at the breakfast table although it was the middle of the morning. Sprog was drinking his third glass of squash because he had done so much talking; Aunt Cis was on her third cup of tea; and So-So was lapping up her third saucer of milk.

Aunt Cis turned over the pages of the morning paper. 'Not a word about Mr. Spruce,' she said. 'Of course, people probably won't believe him – at first. It'll seem such a wild story that no one is going to risk looking foolish by publishing it. Unless, of course, he produces some proof.'

Their eyes fell on the yellow tooth lying on a piece of tissue paper in the centre of the kitchen table.

'The important thing is,' Aunt Cis went on, 'would Mr. Spruce be able to identify you, do you think?'

'He's only seen me once before, when we came out of church,' Sprog reminded her, 'and then he hardly looked at me. He didn't recognise me last night, I'm sure of that. And Talker was well disguised.'

'I'd like to have seen Talker's disguise,' said Aunt Cis pensively.

'The trouble was he was so scared he wouldn't even look at Minerva. It hurt her feelings.'

'Poor Minerva. I'm looking forward to meeting her when she wakes up.'

Sprog frowned. 'I hope she hasn't settled down for one of her long sleeps – you know, a hundred years or so.'

'Perhaps it's only a nap. After all, it was quite an eventful day for her yesterday, having a tooth out and leaving her cave for the first time in several million years. She's probably worn out with the excitement.'

'It may have had something to do with the brandy as well,' said Sprog. 'I don't think she's used to it.'

'Ah, yes . . . the brandy.' Aunt Cis glanced in the direction of the larder and then began to clear away the crockery. 'You know, it wouldn't be a bad idea for Talker to back the car up against the barn doors, so that we can be sure no one can open them. Have you seen him this morning?'

'He's probably still asleep in the car, round the corner in the layby.'

'I think I'll go and ask him to move it now. Then maybe I'll go on down to the shops and see if there are any rumours flying about.'

'Can I come?' asked Sprog, jumping to his feet. 'I'm tired of just sitting around, waiting for something to happen.'

Aunt Cis shook her head. 'No, I think it would be best if you stayed here. We don't want to risk you being seen by Mr. Spruce.'

'He didn't go to work this morning,' said Sprog gloomily, sitting down again. 'I saw his car in the drive. Someone must have driven it round there last night.' He fidgeted impatiently with his empty glass. 'I wish I could be a fly on the wall and see what he's doing now, at this very moment.'

At that very moment a fly on the wall in the Spruces' house would have seen Mr. Spruce in a red silk dressing-gown striding up and down in front of a police constable, who was sitting in an armchair with his notebook on his knee, listening politely.

'I tell you I've absolutely no idea how I came to be smelling of brandy,' Mr. Spruce was saying. 'I'd driven straight home from the surgery.'

'I see,' said the constable. Mrs. Spruce gazed stonily ahead of her.

'The creature smelt of brandy. I suppose some of it may have rubbed off on to me,' suggested Mr. Spruce desperately.

'Indeed it might, sir,' said the constable in a soothing voice. 'Now, this boy . . . this – er, Francis Drake . . . you say you've never seen him before?'

'He was a complete stranger to me. Yet he

knew my name, my son's name . . . and he had my daughter's shoe.'

'You're quite sure it was not your son?'

Mr. Spruce grew scarlet in the face. 'I know my own son, for heaven's sake! What kind of a fool do you think I am?'

'I only mention it, sir, because of the items found in the back of your car – items which all happen to belong to your own children.'

Mr. Spruce sank into the nearest chair and buried his head in his hands. 'If only I had that tooth!' he groaned. 'Then you'd *have* to believe me.'

'Quite so, sir. Perhaps you could describe again for me this *other* person . . . the man who waited outside the cave. I presume it was a man?'

'Yes, yes!' snapped Mr. Spruce. 'At least, I *think* it was a man. It looked rather like a district nurse with a beard.'

'It couldn't, for example, have been a girl dressed up?'

Mr. Spruce raised his head and stared at the policeman. 'Are you still trying to make me think it was one of my own children?' He turned to his wife. 'Ask Jonathan and Caroline to come in here for a moment, will you? Let's get this thing cleared up once and for all!'

Chapter Fifteen

Aunt Cis Meets Minerva

When Aunt Cis returned from the village she put her shopping basket on the table and said, 'A complete blank!'

'Nothing?'

'Not a word.'

'It seems too good to be true!'

'Well, let's not start counting our chickens too soon. These things can build up gradually. Is Minerva awake yet?'

'She wasn't last time I looked. I suppose we ought to give her something to eat.'

'She might as well finish off that rhododendron bush she sat on last night,' Aunt Cis suggested.

They collected the rhododendron bush and entered the barn by the side door.

'Minerva!' called Sprog. 'Are you awake?' He turned to Aunt Cis. 'You do realise, don't you, that you won't hear us talking? It's all done by thought language, but it does work. I can prove it to you.'

'You don't need to prove it to me,' said Aunt Cis. 'I believe you.'

They walked round to the other side of Minerva to see her face, which looked rather endearing in sleep, like an outsize Donald Duck. 'Minerva,' repeated Sprog. 'We've brought you some breakfast.'

Slowly one eye opened and then shut again quickly. 'Oh, my head!' she groaned. 'The light's dazzling me!'

'I expect it's because you're used to living in the dark. I've brought my Aunt Cis to see you.'

Minerva struggled to raise her head and murmured faintly, 'How delightful. So pleased to meet you.'

'She says she's very pleased to meet you,' Sprog translated to Aunt Cis.

'Tell her I'm honoured to make her acquaintance. Shall we shake hands?'

Sprog explained this to Minerva. 'If you reach out your claw she'll put her hand in it. It's the human sign of friendship.'

'What a charming idea!' Minerva clambered to her feet, knocking her head on a rafter as she did so. 'Oooh! I'm sure the world has shrunk! It never used to be this small in the old days.'

'I expect you feel a bit like Gulliver in Lilliput,' said Sprog understandingly. 'Come on, shake hands with Aunt Cis.'

Minerva put out her claw and Aunt Cis pumped it up and down heartily, saying 'How-do-you-do' several times.

'She seems very friendly for a human,' observed Minerva. 'Usually they run away shrieking or cover their eyes, like that rude friend of yours.'

'Or faint, like Mr. Spruce,' said Sprog with a grin.

'That man!' Minerva shuddered. 'I do so agree with you about dentists.'

'How's your jaw this morning?' he inquired. 'It doesn't look so swollen.'

She took a moment to consider. 'Much better,' she admitted. 'It still hurts a little, but not nearly so much as it did.'

'Let's have a look.'

Minerva opened her mouth and he peered in. So did Aunt Cis. Sprog pointed out to her the hole where the tooth had been.

'Looks healthy enough to me,' said Aunt Cis.

'But the cotton wool's gone.' He looked up at Minerva. 'Did you swallow it?'

'I may have done. I do have a slight touch of indigestion.' Minerva eyed the rhododendron bush. 'Is that for me?'

'Yes, it's your breakfast. You knocked it down last night so Aunt Cis says you may as well have it.'

'How kind.' Tears came into Minerva's eyes. 'You're spoiling me! I shall eat it very slowly and make it last.' She began chewing one twig so deliberately it was like watching a film in slow motion.

'I think,' said Sprog to Aunt Cis, 'she's got used to not eating much over the years because it was so difficult for her to get food.'

Aunt Cis nodded. 'She's had to adapt, poor creature. I suppose she's eaten all the vegetation around the cave opening but dared not come out too far for fear of the Tyrant King.'

'I feel waves of sympathy coming towards me from your aunt,' Minerva remarked suddenly. 'I like her. She reminds me very much of my own dear Auntie, who fled north to escape Tyrant King. I fear she may have perished in that terrible winter—'

'You mean the Ice Age,' said Sprog.

'Most likely. But she had much the same look about her as your Aunt Cis – so practical and good at looking after people. Dear thing!' And Minerva gave Aunt Cis an approving pat on the shoulder which almost knocked her over.

Meanwhile, Mr. Spruce was trying to convince the doctor that his temperature was perfectly normal, but he was not making himself very clear as he still had the thermometer in his mouth.

'Just sit quietly,' said the doctor, taking hold of Mr. Spruce's wrist.

'My pulse is normal too!' protested Mr. Spruce between closed lips, like a ventriloquist.

The doctor frowned. 'A little rapid, but nothing too alarming.' He glanced at Mrs. Spruce, who was hovering anxiously. 'Has he ever experienced anything like this before?'

'No, I haven't!' shouted Mr. Spruce.

With a resigned sigh the doctor picked up the thermometer from the carpet.

'And I'll tell you *why* I haven't,' went on Mr. Spruce forcefully. 'Because nothing like this has ever happened to *anybody* before! What can I say to convince you?' He jumped to his feet and began pacing up and down. 'There is, living among the Tibor Rocks, a dinosaur. One of the duck-billed dinosaurs with a crested head, to be more exact. I think it's a corythosaurus, although I haven't had time to check it yet. Now, I've no idea how it's survived, but nonetheless it's there – I've seen it with my own eyes. All I ask is for someone else to go up there and investigate.'

'The police *have* been up there, dear,' said Mrs. Spruce, 'and they weren't able to find anything.'

'They haven't made a proper search. They need expert help. The caves must be explored again, starting with the one they call Dragon's Tooth Cave. Now, *that* tooth has never been satisfactorily explained either! I'm going to see the Vicar. I want to have another look at the tooth in his museum . . .'

Mrs. Spruce put a detaining hand on his arm. 'Don't you think you should rest?'

He threw off her arm and strode out of the room.

Mrs. Spruce turned appealingly to the doctor, who shook his head. 'Let him go. I'll give you a prescription for some sedatives.'

'But what's wrong with him, Doctor? Is it overwork?'

The doctor looked doubtful. 'It's an interesting case,' he admitted. 'There's a man I'd like him to see – a specialist.'

Mrs. Spruce turned pale. 'You mean, a psychiatrist?'

'Just a friend of mine who happens to be staying with me at present,' said the doctor reassuringly. 'May I use your telephone?'

'Please do.' She went out of the room, leaving the doctor to make his call, and found her children waiting in the hall.

'Where's Daddy gone?'

'What's happening?'

'Has he gone mad?'

Mrs. Spruce raised her hand to quell the babble. 'Quiet, children, please! There's absolutely nothing to worry about. Your father has had an unpleasant experience, but he's perfectly all right. I'm sure we shall soon get the whole thing sorted out.'

'Is that why the police asked us about the dressing-up clothes?' persisted Jonathan.

'They even asked me about my shoe,' said Caroline, 'but I've no idea how it got into Daddy's car, honestly!'

'Oh, dear!' Mrs. Spruce pressed a hand to her forehead and said faintly, 'I've the most dreadful headache coming on again. I think I'll just go and make myself a cup of tea.'

'We wouldn't lie to the police,' Jonathan called after her. 'We're not *that* stupid.'

'It must have been a burglar,' said Caroline, nervously twisting the ends of her long hair around her fingers.

Only Charlotte kept silent.

Chapter Sixteen

A Family Joke?

'I can't see the front door from here,' said Sprog, peering out of the hayloft window, 'but I've a good view of the drive. Hey, what do you think? Mr. Spruce had just gone racing out of the gate and up the road!'

'Let me have a look,' said Minerva, craning her long neck up the steps, while the rest of her stayed down below with Aunt Cis.

'I don't think you can see him now. He's out of sight.' Sprog moved aside to make room for her.

'What's going on?' Aunt Cis called up the steps.

'Nothing much. Oh, yes . . . the doctor's leaving. And I can see Jonathan and the two girls . . . they've just come out into the garden. They seem to be having an argument.'

'Hang on, I think we've got a visitor,' said Aunt Cis. The door banged behind her.

'You'd better move your head out of the way and let me go down,' said Sprog to Minerva. 'I want to find out what's happening.'

He found Aunt Cis in the kitchen with the police constable he had met at Tibor Rocks the previous evening.

'Just the young man I wanted to see!' exclaimed the policeman as Sprog came through the door. He turned to Aunt Cis. 'Have you any objections to my asking your grand-nephew a few questions, ma'am?'

'None at all,' said Aunt Cis calmly.

'Now then, my lad,' he began. 'When I met you up by the caves last night I asked you if you'd seen anything odd and you said no. I suppose you wouldn't have remembered anything else since then . . . anything at all out of the ordinary?'

Sprog looked puzzled. 'No, I'm afraid not.'

'Then I've only one other question.' The policeman looked a little embarrassed. 'Do you ever play with the children next-door-but-one . . . that's Mr. Spruce's house?'

'I know, the dentist,' said Sprog. 'I've met them once or twice.' He looked to Aunt Cis for help.

'I introduced him to the Spruce children after church last Sunday,' she explained. 'I thought they might be good company for him, but it didn't work out quite as I'd hoped. It appears the boy – Jonathan, I think his name is – wasn't prepared to be friendly.'

'We had a fight,' said Sprog frankly.

The policeman gave an understanding nod. 'You've never been inside their house, then?'

Now, if there was one thing Sprog did not want to do, it was to lie to the police, so he answered the question with a half-truth. 'I've been in the drive,' he said. 'One of the girls shut herself in the shed and I let her out. Then Jonathan came along and said I was trespassing. That's when we had the fight.'

'I see.' The policeman looked doubtful. 'You wouldn't by any chance have a grudge against the family, would you? On account of this fight, I mean.'

'Of course not,' Sprog assured him. 'I don't even know them, really.'

The constable turned to Aunt Cis. 'Well, I'm sorry to have troubled you, ma'am. Just routine inquiries, you know.'

'Of course,' murmured Aunt Cis, adding in a low voice as she showed him to the front door, 'Is there trouble of some kind?'

'Nothing serious,' he said in the same low tone. 'To be honest, I suspect something in the nature of a family joke, but we have to check up on these things. I hope I haven't alarmed your little lad.'

'I doubt it,' said Aunt Cis.

She closed the door behind him and returned to the kitchen.

Sprog said thoughtfully, 'You know, I can't help feeling we ought to wait a while before taking Minerva back to her cave, just in case someone eventually believes Mr. Spruce and goes to have a closer look.'

'I agree,' said Aunt Cis. 'The danger isn't over yet.'

When Mr. Spruce returned from the Vicarage he found his wife waiting for him in the sitting-room with the doctor and a small round man with a bald head.

'This is my friend, Mr. Herman Steinbeck,' said the doctor.

Mr. Spruce ignored Mr. Steinbeck's outstretched hand. 'I was absolutely right!' he announced. 'The tooth in the museum is identical to the one I extracted last night – the same irregular shape, the same thick coating of enamel on the outside edge. . . . And it was a corythosaurus, as I said. I looked it up. The Vicar's inclined to be sceptical, but he's getting in touch

with a couple of local cave divers. I want them to make a thorough search of that cave, so we're meeting at the 'George and Dragon' for lunch and then going on up to Tibor Rocks.'

The doctor patted him on the shoulder. 'That sounds like an excellent idea,' he said. 'Don't you agree, Herman?'

Mr. Steinbeck nodded wisely. 'Coming to grips with one's fears . . . having the courage to face one's nightmares in the daylight . . . that is always the best course.'

Mr. Spruce stared at the stranger. 'What are you?' he asked rudely. 'Are you a shrink or something?'

Mr. Steinbeck looked annoyed. 'It so happens I specialise in paranormal psychological disturbances . . .'

'Well, I've no idea what that might be,' interrupted Mr. Spruce, 'but as far as I'm concerned you can go take a running jump! There's nothing wrong with my mind, do you understand?' He glared round at all of them. 'I'm perfectly sane and I'm going to prove it to you beyond any shadow of doubt.'

'Fascinating,' murmured Mr. Steinbeck. 'But surely you wouldn't mind telling me about it? I'm quite prepared to believe you, but I'd like to hear the facts for myself.'

Mr. Spruce looked slightly less angry. 'Oh, well . . . if you're really interested . . .'

'I am, I am!' Mr. Steinbeck assured him earnestly.

Mr. Spruce glanced at his watch. 'There are a few moments before I'm due at the "George and Dragon". Take a seat . . .'

Mr. Steinbeck sat down, his eyes fixed on Mr. Spruce's face. Mrs. Spruce let out a sigh of relief and the doctor gave her an encouraging smile.

'Now,' urged Mr. Steinbeck, 'supposing you tell me all about it?'

Chapter Seventeen

A Close Shave

Sprog looked through the window of the Morris which was backed up against the doors of the barn. Talker sat in the driving seat with his hands on the wheel and his chin resting on his chest, snoring gently.

'Talker,' said Sprog, giving him a little push. 'Aunt Cis wants to know if you're going to sit out here all day?'

'Eh? What?' Talker opened his eyes and blinked. 'Tell her I'm happier out here if she don't mind. Any sign of trouble back there,' he jerked his head in the direction of the barn, 'and I shall be off like a flea at the races.'

Sprog sighed. He was just about to go into the barn to keep Minerva company for a while when he heard voices. Creeping round the side of the house he saw the three Spruce children standing outside Dolphin Cottage, arguing fiercely.

'I don't want to!' That was Charley's voice.

'And I say you must!' Jonathan sounded impatient. 'Go and knock at the door. We'll be here, listening to every word he says.'

Sprog flattened himself against the wall, straining his ears to catch their conversation. If the Spruces intended to march in and ask him if he had taken their dressing-up clothes this could turn out to be a very tricky situation indeed.

'I'm not going in *there*!' Charley was protesting tearfully. 'That witch might turn me into a – frog or something.'

'She's not a witch, stupid. Anyway, we'll be right behind you.'

Caroline said something quietly to her brother. Sprog could only just make out her words of caution. '. . . ought to be careful. After all, Mummy did say it was Susan Barnes. She spoke to her.'

There was a pause and then Jonathan said sternly, 'Look here, Charlotte, if this is one of your fairy stories you'd better own up now. Otherwise we're going to look like complete idiots.'

At this Charley burst noisily into tears. 'I hate you, Jonathan. You can't make me go into that house if I don't want to. I'm going to tell

Mummy what a bully you are!' The sound of her sobs grew fainter as she ran back up the road.

Caroline sighed. 'I told you she was making it all up. It's just as well we didn't go in there accusing that boy of taking our things.'

'I suppose so,' Jonathan agreed gloomily. 'Pity, though. I was rather looking forward to a good scrap.'

'Never mind,' said his sister. 'We'd better go home and see if that doctor has managed to calm Daddy down a bit.'

As their voices retreated up the road Sprog let out a long sigh of relief and went straight into the kitchen to tell Aunt Cis what a narrow escape they had just had.

A hush had fallen on the bar at the 'George and Dragon'. Mr. Spruce held the centre of the floor, his expression eager, his hair ruffled where he kept scratching his head, trying to puzzle out a way to convince the cave divers that what he was telling them was fact and not some impossible fiction.

'I tell you, I can prove it!' he argued. 'There'll be tracks . . . a creature as large as that must leave some traces of her existence.'

'Oh, so it's a "her", is it?' inquired the land-lord, leaning over the bar.

'The boy called it Minerva,' said Mr. Spruce shortly. 'He said he could talk to her.'

Silence again. The landlord hid a smile and one of the cavers dug his companion in the ribs.

Mr. Spruce saw he was on dangerous ground. 'I know it sounds fantastic, but I assure you I'm not the sort of man who goes around making up tall stories just so that people can laugh at him!'

The first caver cleared his throat. 'I suppose this – er, creature – couldn't have been a model of some kind?'

'Not a chance,' retorted Mr. Spruce. 'It was alive and breathing all right. It opened its mouth when the boy told it to and when I took the tooth out there was blood.'

The landlord chuckled. 'Blow me if this don't beat even old Talker's stories about the dragon.'

Mr. Spruce sighed impatiently. 'Don't you understand? All those stories about the dragon must have been sparked off by the presence of this dinosaur in the caves. It explains everything!'

One or two people began to look embarrassed and turned away. Mr. Steinbeck, who had been standing behind Mr. Spruce, taking notes, tapped him on the shoulder. 'Shall we go home now?' he suggested. 'Your wife will be getting anxious.' He took hold of Mr. Spruce's arm.

Mr. Spruce shook him off angrily. 'Not yet! I've some business to discuss with these two young men.' He turned to the cavers and took out his wallet. 'I'm prepared to pay you well to make a proper search of the Dragon's Tooth Cave.' He waved an impressive wad of notes in front of their eyes. 'I'll give you cash now, to dive. But if you find anything – another cave, another tooth – anything that helps to prove me right, then you'll find me very generous indeed!'

The cavers looked uncertain. The wad of notes was tempting.

'What have you got to lose?' persisted Mr. Spruce.

The first caver shrugged. 'Okay,' he said, glancing at his friend, who nodded. 'We'll do it.'

Chapter Eighteen

Mr. Spruce Appears on Television

'She's getting cramped in the barn,' said Sprog to Aunt Cis, when he returned from keeping Minerva company in the afternoon. 'She says it doesn't seem nearly so large as it did when she first arrived. I'm afraid she's getting restless.'

'Well, she'll have to stay there for the time being,' said Aunt Cis. 'I've just seen an expedition making its way up to Tibor Rocks, led by Mr. Spruce.'

Sprog stared at her. 'You mean he's actually got someone to believe him?'

'It looks like it. There are cavers there with their diving equipment, a photographer and quite a crowd of onlookers. One of them was a reporter from the local paper.'

'I knew this would happen!' said Sprog

despairingly. 'Supposing they find the other tunnel? She'll *never* be able to go back. Shall we have to give her up?'

'Over my dead body,' said his aunt. 'We'll find a home for her somewhere else, if necessary.'

Sprog sighed. 'I can't help thinking it must be terribly lonely, being the only dinosaur left in the world.'

'She may not be. After all, if she's managed to survive so long undetected, why not others?' Aunt Cis got to her feet.

'Where are you going?'

'Up to the cave, to mingle with the crowd and find out what's happening. You'd better not come, in case Mr. Spruce sees you.'

He sat down glumly at the table. 'This waiting around is getting on my nerves.'

'Why don't you take the television set over to Minerva?' Aunt Cis suggested. 'I don't suppose she's ever seen anything like that before. At least it'll keep her amused.'

'That's a good idea,' said Sprog, cheering up a little.

By late afternoon Mrs. Spruce had resigned herself to sitting beside the telephone, one hand poised over the receiver and a glass of water in the other. A bottle of aspirin stood on the table.

'This has been the most exciting day of my life!' said Jonathan. He and Caroline were standing by the window, watching the small crowd gathering outside in the drive. 'I *knew* Dad wasn't making it up. I said so all along.'

'Ssssh, children,' said Mrs. Spruce wearily. 'Where's Charlotte?'

'Upstairs in her room, sulking,' Jonathan replied. 'She still thinks we're blaming her for the whole thing. She hasn't heard the latest news.'

The telephone rang shrilly and Mrs. Spruce snatched up the receiver. 'Hello, yes? I'm afraid my husband is rather busy at the moment, making a statement to the Press.' There was a long pause. 'Oh, I see. Yes, I'll try and get him to come to the 'phone. Jonathan, go and see if your father can spare a minute to speak to BBC Television, will you?'

Jonathan dashed across the hall and into the study, which was packed with people. ''Scuse me,' he said, elbowing his way through a group of young men with notebooks.

'Are you the son? What's your name, kid? Do you believe in dinosaurs?' A few flashlights went off.

'Dad, Dad!' he shouted, pushing aside Mr. Steinbeck, who was also writing in his notebook. 'Mum says you've got to come to the telephone.

It's important.'

By now Mr. Spruce was growing tired of repeating his story over and over again. 'I'll have a statement typed out,' he announced, raising his voice above the din. He looked down at his son. 'What is it, Jonathan?'

'The BBC. They want to talk to you.'

'Just coming. Excuse me, gentlemen. I shan't keep you waiting long.' He followed Jonathan into the sitting room and ordered him to lock the door. 'Phew! Those chaps are certainly persistent. What's this about, then?'

Mrs. Spruce handed him the receiver.

'Hello, Spruce here,' he said briskly. 'That's right. . . . Yes, I know it's difficult to believe, but it happens to be true.' He winked at his son. 'They've discovered a huge great sump they never even knew existed, leading into an enormous chamber. There are plenty of signs that a creature has been living there – half-eaten silver birches, you know the kind of thing . . . That's right – an extraction . . . Yes, it was a terrifying experience, but quite frankly I was too fascinated at the time to be frightened . . . This evening?' He glanced at his watch. 'Yes, I suppose I could. At your Bristol studio? Yes, I know where it is. Right, then. Goodbye.'

He replaced the receiver and looked round

triumphantly at his family. 'This is it! We're about to be famous!'

'Oh dear!' said Mrs. Spruce, reaching for the aspirin. 'I hope it isn't going to make us look foolish.'

Her husband shot her an impatient look. 'Of course it won't! They'll find the creature, don't worry. It can't escape, not something that big. An organised search of the entire Mendips has already started.'

'I can't feel my left hind leg!' said Minerva. 'Except for a strange tingling sensation.'

'Pins and needles,' Sprog told her. 'It's because you're all cramped up. Try turning round a little.'

She moved a few inches and knocked down a shelf, scattering tools and oil cans on to the floor. Sprog bent to pick them up.

'I want to go home,' she sniffed.

'That's impossible,' said Sprog. 'There are masses of people around the cave. Aunt Cis says they're determined to capture you and they've got all sorts of things to help them, like a hypodermic dart to fire into you which would send you to sleep.'

'I wish I'd never woken up in the first place,' she grumbled. 'I don't like this new world. It's far too cluttered up with people and buildings. It was much nicer when it was empty.'

'You mustn't get depressed. Shall we watch the television again? There may be a better programme on now.'

'We ought to watch the News,' said Aunt Cis, entering the barn at that moment. 'Just in case . . .'

Sprog switched on the television.

'And finally,' said the newsreader, allowing himself a slight smile, 'it looks as if England may have found its own answer to the Loch Ness monster. Mr. Christopher Spruce, a Bristol dentist, announced last night that he had extracted a tooth from a dinosaur he found alive and well and living in a cave in the Mendip Hills. Our reporter is talking to Mr. Spruce in our Bristol studio.'

Suddenly Mr. Spruce appeared on the screen, looking rather smug. The reporter asked him some questions, which he answered with calm assurance.

'But you haven't actually been able to find this boy – or, indeed, the dinosaur itself?'

Mr. Spruce admitted he had not.

'Doesn't it seem more likely to you that the whole thing was an elaborate practical joke?'

'Certainly not,' said Mr. Spruce firmly. 'It

was quite real, I assure you.'

'Then where is the dinosaur now?'

'I'm convinced it won't be long before we find it. A full-scale search is under way. We've already found an entirely new tunnel, together with traces of the creature's existence. It has to be around somewhere.'

'But isn't it a rather frightening thought for people living in that area that this – er, creature might be roaming around the countryside? Aren't you in danger of alarming a great many people unnecessarily?'

'I don't think there's much danger attached,' said Mr. Spruce confidently. 'It is in fact a corythosaurus – a plant-eating dinosaur. It isn't interested in human flesh.'

'Ah, yes. We have a picture of a corythosaurus coming up on our screens right now. Is that your dinosaur, Mr. Spruce?'

Minerva blinked. 'That's exactly like *me*!' she said to Sprog.

'Yes, that's the one,' said Mr. Spruce.

'Thank you, Mr. Spruce.' The reporter turned to face the camera. 'And now, just to put the record straight, perhaps we'd better remind you what the Loch Ness monster looks like . . .'

A somewhat blurred picture came on to the screen. Minerva sat up with such speed that she hit her head on the roof of the barn.

'Auntie!' she cried in a glad voice, and the tears began to roll down her cheeks.

Chapter Nineteen

Preparing for the Journey

'We can't possibly drive up to Scotland tonight,' said Aunt Cis, sitting down beside the telephone. 'There simply isn't time to make all the arrangements. I suppose Minerva *is* right? There doesn't seem to be much family resemblance between her and the Loch Ness monster.'

'She says it wasn't her real Auntie, just a friend of the family,' Sprog explained. 'They united to fight Tyrant King and then when things got too bad this Auntie went up north. Minerva's very excited about seeing her again.'

Aunt Cis picked up the telephone and dialled a number. 'It would certainly solve the problem, although getting her there isn't going to be easy. Hello,' she said into the receiver. 'Is that you, George? This is Cissie Stokes speaking. Look,

I'm sorry to bother you, but I want to get a very long load up to Scotland as soon as possible. Can you help? What? Oh, about nine metres, I should think. Hang on a moment.' She covered the mouthpiece with her hand. 'He says he can let us have a trailer with a tarpaulin, but I don't think that'll do, do you? I mean, a dinosaur covered with a tarpaulin is going to look pretty suspicious. Even if we travel at night it would be too risky.'

'And she might fall off,' Sprog pointed out.

'Exactly,' She uncovered the mouthpiece. 'George, have you got some kind of a container? How high is it?' Looking doubtful, she put her hand over the receiver again. 'It's going to be an awful squash. She'll have to lie on her side. Do you think she could manage that for about twelve hours?'

'We can give her something to make her sleep.'

'That's a good idea.' She spoke into the receiver. 'That would suit us very well. Could we possibly borrow it tomorrow evening for about thirty-six hours? Oh, that *is* kind of you. Yes, Talker Harris will collect it at about six o'clock. Thanks very much indeed. Goodbye.' She replaced the receiver.

Sprog looked impressed. 'They must think a lot of you, letting you have a truck just like that.'

'My brother and his wife took George into their home when he was quite small,' she explained, 'and since they had no children of their own George eventually inherited my brother's road haulage business. I knew he'd help us.'

'But will Talker be able to manage a truck like that?' asked Sprog doubtfully.

'I sincerely hope so!' said Aunt Cis, with feeling. 'He's going to have to drive pretty fast. I reckon the journey – even taking the most direct route we can find and making no stops except absolutely essential ones – must take us twelve hours at least, and we want to travel as much as possible in the dark.'

Sprog worked it out in his head. 'So we should reach Loch Ness about seven o'clock the next morning?' He frowned anxiously. 'What if her Auntie doesn't recognise her after all these years? Or supposing she doesn't even exist? What will Minerva do?'

'I think that's a risk we have to take,' said Aunt Cis seriously. 'We've really no choice. Minerva will never be able to return to her cave now. No, Scotland is our only hope.'

Sprog sighed. 'I'd better go and tell her about it.'

He found Minerva with her neck stretched up into the loft, gazing out at the darkness.

'Lights everywhere,' she murmured. 'It's really rather pretty.'

'Those are torches,' he told her. 'People are out looking for you.'

'For me?' She was surprised. 'Why should they go to all that bother, just for me?'

Sprog saw that it was useless trying to convince her of her own danger, so instead he told her of their plan to take her to Scotland.

'To see Auntie again?' breathed Minerva.

'We hope so,' he said cautiously. 'That is, if it *was* her you saw on television.'

'Oh, that was definitely Auntie! I'd know her anywhere.' Tears gathered in her eyes. 'I'm so happy, Sprog, I don't know how to thank you!' She held out a claw and he patted it awkwardly, trying to suppress his doubts that they were doing the right thing by taking her so far away from her old home.

During the night they moved the car forward and opened the barn doors so that Minerva could have a stretch, but they dared not leave them open. The whole of Mendip seemed astir. There had been reported sightings of the creature all over the county and even further afield.

The next morning Silverton hit the headlines in three daily newspapers and was even given a mention in *The Times*. 'Tongue-in-cheek,' said Aunt Cis. 'They don't really believe in it.'

'There's a picture here of Mr. Spruce with his mouth open,' said Sprog.

Talker groaned and refused to look. 'I'm not setting foot outside this door today,' he said. 'Everyone's bound to ask me what I think. I'm supposed to be the expert on dragons around here.'

'I agree with you, Talker,' said Aunt Cis. 'It would be far better if you stay here today and sleep as much as possible so that you're wide awake tonight for the drive north.'

'I haven't had much practice at handling them twelve-gear jobs lately,' he grumbled. 'It's going to be a long haul.'

'But you can do it, Talker,' said Aunt Cis firmly. 'Why don't you get some rest now, in the sitting room?'

When he had disappeared she said to Sprog, 'The next thing we must work out is how we're going to load Minerva on to the truck without anyone seeing.'

'Especially that reporter who keeps walking up and down the road asking people questions,' said Sprog. 'I think he's waiting for something to happen.'

'We'll have to create some kind of a diversion,'

said Aunt Cis. 'Just before Talker's due back here with the truck I'll rush out of the house as if I've just had a message to go up to Tibor Rocks urgently. With any luck the reporter will follow me – and half the village as well, I shouldn't wonder. That's when you load Minerva on to the truck and wait for me to come back. Have you given her the sleeping pills?'

Sprog nodded. 'A whole bottleful.'

'Good. That should keep her quiet for a while.'

At last it was time for Talker to go and collect the truck. The Morris set off with its usual bangs and fireworks, which brought the reporter running down the road to see if he was missing

anything. When he saw the ancient car disappearing round the corner he turned away, disappointed.

'Now all we can do is wait for Talker's signal,' said Aunt Cis.

At five minutes to seven the telephone bell rang three times and then stopped. 'There it is!' said Aunt Cis, and she hurried out of Dolphin Cottage, almost knocking over the reporter who was leaning against a lamp post.

'What's up?' he called after her.

Aunt Cis broke into a trot. 'Can't stop,' she said over her shoulder. 'Urgent message . . . Tibor Rocks.'

The people of Silverton were already nervous and poised for action. The sound of running footsteps brought them to their gates.

'Urgent message,' gasped the reporter. 'Up to the caves. . . .'

Arming themselves with umbrellas and pick-axes, the people of Silverton began to march up the hill behind the valiant figure of Aunt Cis.

Meanwhile Talker was carefully backing the truck into the drive. He got out of the cab, wiping the sweat from his brow. 'Fantastic job, this!' he said, his eyes alight with enthusiasm.

'It looks pretty large,' said Sprog thankfully.

'Let's get Minerva loaded straight away.'

This was not an easy operation, partly because Talker insisted on keeping his eyes firmly closed and partly because Minerva was reluctant to enter the truck. 'It doesn't look very comfortable,' she complained.

'You'll be asleep in no time. Those were sleeping pills I gave you.'

The tears were beginning to roll again. 'It was cosy in my little cave.'

Sprog said encouragingly, 'Think of your Auntie. She'll be so pleased to see you. I expect she's been as lonely up there in the loch as you have, down here in your cave.'

Minerva shook her head. 'There's something . . . I can't quite remember what it is, but there's some good reason why I ought not to leave that cave.'

'There's an even better reason why you should! Please hurry. Aunt Cis will be back in a minute.'

Slowly she began to move forward. 'I trust you, Sprog,' she said, as a large tear splashed on to the ground. 'I'll do whatever you say.'

He breathed a sigh of relief as she clambered into the truck. Talker helped him close up the back, while keeping his eyes resolutely turned away. The road outside was still deserted.

'I reckon the whole village must have followed Aunt Cis,' said Sprog as he climbed into the cab. 'I wonder if she's managed to give them the slip.'

Talker was too busy playing with the gears to reply.

At last Aunt Cis appeared, breathless but triumphant. 'I took the short cut,' she panted. 'Hundreds of people up there, all running in different directions. They didn't even notice when I left.'

'We're all ready,' Sprog told her. 'Minerva's crying but she's lying down and should be asleep soon. We've got the food and the thermos.'

'What about the map?'

They had forgotten the map, so Aunt Cis dashed back into Dolphin Cottage to collect it. She soon reappeared, locking the door behind her, and climbed into the cab. 'Right, Talker! Off we go, on the road to Scotland . . .'

Chapter Twenty

Reunion

By the time they reached the motorway Talker had mastered the gears and was enjoying himself enormously. He began singing all sorts of travelling songs in a rough, untuneful baritone which made sleep or conversation impossible, so both Sprog and Aunt Cis sat silent, occupied with their own thoughts.

They drove monotonously on, mile after mile. At length Talker's voice gave out and there was no sound except the droning of the engine. Sprog's head drooped against Aunt Cis's shoulder. He never noticed the passing of Birmingham or Carlisle and stirred only momentarily just before Edinburgh, when they stopped to give Talker another break.

They were between Perth and Inverness when he finally awoke, feeling cold and stiff. 'What's the time?' he murmured, moving his cramped arms and legs.

'Six o'clock,' said his aunt. 'You've slept most of the journey away.'

'Have you been asleep too?'

'No, I've been navigating, as well as chatting to Talker to keep him awake. We should be in Inverness soon after seven.'

'But it'll be light by then!'

'Probably. It's still early, though. I think we ought to take the road along the eastern shore, towards Foyers. Then we'll stop wherever we see a suitable place.'

They drove along the shores of Loch Ness without speaking. It was the first time Sprog had ever been to Scotland, yet he found no pleasure in looking at the beautiful wooded hills and distant moorland. His eyes were drawn again and again to the dark, unfriendly waters of the loch, and he could think only of Minerva sinking beneath the depths to find no welcoming Auntie but instead a serpentine monster more dreadful than Tyrant King.

He shivered and said to Aunt Cis, 'I wish we hadn't brought her here.'

She nodded understandingly. 'When she goes into the water we'll wait for a while to make sure everything's all right.'

'If it doesn't work out we could always take her back again, I suppose. Even the British Museum would be better than . . .' His voice tailed off unhappily.

'Here, don't tell me we've had all this journey for nothing!' protested Talker. 'I'm not taking that thing back to Silverton again!'

'It probably won't be necessary,' said Aunt Cis soothingly. 'Look over there, Talker – there's a good spot. You can pull off the road.'

They stopped and got down from the cab. Everything seemed silent and eerie in the morning mist.

Aunt Cis put a hand to her aching back. 'I think Talker and I should go about a hundred metres along the road in different directions, so that if a car comes along we can stop it on some pretext or other.'

Talker seemed only too happy to agree, since it gave him a good excuse not to be around when Minerva came out of the truck. He helped Sprog unfasten the back and then almost ran back along the road.

'Can you manage by yourself now?' asked aunt Cis.

Sprog nodded and she set off in the opposite direction to Talker.

Left on his own he touched Minerva lightly on

the hind leg. She raised her head and asked sleepily, 'Have we arrived? Thank goodness for that. Is Auntie there?'

'Not yet. You'll have to call her.'

With some difficulty she emerged backwards from the truck and looked about her. 'My goodness!' she exclaimed when she saw the loch. 'What a large pool!' She made for the bank and stretched her neck down towards the water. 'This is more like the world I remember.' She lifted her head and sniffed the air. 'Yes, I like it . . . I like it very much!'

'Oh, good!' Sprog began to feel better. 'I was afraid you . . .'

'Sssh! I'm listening.'

They stood in silence while Minerva extended her neck over the water. At last she said, 'I can hear something.'

'Minerva, you will take care!'

'Yes, yes,' she said impatiently, and plopped into the water before Sprog had time to realise what she was doing.

'Minerva!' he shouted. 'I want to know what happens.'

She turned round to face him. 'Of course, dear friend. Did you really think I'd leave you without saying goodbye? Anyway, it's not goodbye. You're going to come and see me, aren't you?'

He said miserably, 'I *may* be able to. But Scotland's a long way away.'

'I must go – someone's calling.' She began swimming towards the centre of the loch.

'Be careful!'

But she was already too intent upon something else. He watched her swimming strongly, only her head and the hump of her back showing, with an occasional lash from her tail disturbing the water.

After a few moments he thought he could make out another dark shape beside her, just below the surface. With a sudden dive she disappeared and the loch became calm. For what seemed like ages he waited, his eyes fixed to the spot where he had last seen her. His heart was thumping wildly. What was happening in the depths of those dark waters?

At last he saw her head appear. She was swimming towards him and then stopped about twenty metres from the shore. Her words came very faintly into his mind. 'Mustn't come any farther . . .'

'Is it all right?' he asked. 'Is she really your Auntie?'

'Wonderful . . . welcome . . .' came the answer.

'Are you going to stay?'

'For ever . . .' Her head disappeared for a moment and then came up again. 'Must go. Auntie says . . . not safe . . .'

'No, you go. Go quickly!'

Long after the loch was still and silent again he went on looking. Then he remembered Aunt Cis and Talker and he went to the cab of the truck to sound the horn as a signal that all was clear.

While he was waiting for them he went on

looking at the water and was eventually re-
warded by the sight of a skinny arm waving at
him from the centre of the loch. He strained to
catch what she was saying but could only pick
up the odd word. Then she was gone again.

'What happened?' asked Aunt Cis as she came
towards him. 'Is she all right?'

'I think so,' said Sprog. 'She met her Auntie
and they went off together, but just now she
came up again, in the centre of the loch.
She tried to tell me something, but I couldn't
understand it. Something about a ledge and a
crack . . .'

'Maybe there's a ledge down there, and a
crack – possibly even a cave,' Aunt Cis suggested. 'She was describing her new home, I
expect.'

'That might be it,' he agreed doubtfully.

'Are you happy now, Sprog? Do you want to
stay any longer?'

He shook his head. 'No, I'm sure it's all right.
I felt it. She was very happy.'

'Good. Then we can leave her with a clear
conscience. Oh, here comes Talker.'

The old man came limping towards them.
'Can we go now? I'm hungry.'

Aunt Cis beamed at him. 'And you have
earned the largest breakfast money can buy,

Talker! Shall we go back to Inverness?'

'Sooner the better,' said Talker, climbing into the cab.

The Dragon's Tooth Cave was packed with sightseers, as well as the Vicar who was hoping to find another tooth to go with the one he already had, and Mr. Spruce who was being photographed for an article in the *Dental Gazette*.

Along the sump there was a group of divers engaged in a survey of Scroggins Cave, so called after the caver who was the first to enter it, much to the annoyance of Mr. Spruce, who thought it should have been named after him.

But strangely enough, in all their searchings, none of them noticed that high on a ledge, lay an egg, about twenty centimetres in length, with a ridged and wrinkled shell. A shell that had just begun to crack . . .